D1625404

Date Due

A week or so before summer ended one of the guys back home asked me why I had decided on Winslow School in the first place. I don't remember what I answered exactly, but the question stuck because I never imagined anyone asking. I'd be willing to bet a pair of Top-Siders that most Winslow boys would have been as surprised as I was.

The place is a Preppie Hall of Fame. Becoming a Winslow boy sets you apart. It doesn't mean you're better than anyone else; it just means you have a better chance at everything. Which amounts to the same thing.

Right?

Wrong?

Maybe.

Anyway, I went.

STEPHEN ROOS is the author of *The Incredible Cat Caper*, written with Kelley Roos, *My Horrible Secret, The Terrible Truth*, and *My Secret Admirer*, all available in Dell Yearling editions. He divides his time between Ulster County, New York, and Key West, Florida.

ALSO AVAILABLE IN LAUREL-LEAF BOOKS:

Confessions

of a

Wayward

Preppie

STEPHEN ROOS

25462

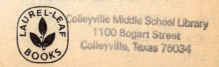

LAUREL-LEAF BOOKS bring together under a single imprint outstanding works of fiction and nonfiction particularly suitable for young adult readers, both in and out of the classroom. Charles F. Reasoner, Professor Emeritus of Children's Literature and Reading, New York University, is consultant to this series.

Published by
Dell Publishing Co., Inc.
1 Dag Hammarskjold Plaza
New York, New York 10017

Laurel-Leaf Library ® TM 766734, Dell Publishing Co., Inc.

ISBN: 0-440-91586-4

RL: 6.2

Reprinted by arrangement with Delacorte Press

Printed in the United States of America

November 1987

10 9 8 7 6 5 4 3 2 1

WFH

For Michelle Poploff

Chapter 1

My father was late. Through the French doors that led from the lobby of Main to the driveway, I saw the Winslow School van take off with the last of the boys who were going to the railroad station. A limousine pulled up through the gate and stopped. The chauffeur got out and walked to the door, dodging the snowflakes that were falling lightly.

Bobby rose from the bench where we were sitting. He picked up his suitcases and handed them to the driver.

"See you around, Carmichael," he said. "Try to take it easy over vacation, okay?"

"Yeah," I said. "You have a nice Christmas."

Bobby followed the chauffeur out of the French doors and got into the car. I watched the limousine turn the corner by the pond and head for the interstate.

I was alone now. The other boys were all gone, and the doors to the faculty offices were closed. Most of the masters left Winslow for the holidays too. I watched the last of the snowflakes fall. There was a foot of snow on the ground, and ice hung from the trees. Everything was still and silent.

Footsteps clicking along in the hall broke the quiet. I looked up. It was Mr. Grady. Very thin, very tall, and very gray. Today he looked weary too.

"Your father not here yet?" he asked.

I shook my head. "Probably the snow."

"He shouldn't be too long," Mr. Grady said. "I'm sorry about what happened, Cary. I truly mean that."

"Me too," I said.

"I wanted you to know I didn't have any choice in the matter," he said.

"I don't blame you if that's what you mean," I said.

"And next year," he said. "Well, next year's another year. It'll work out better for you. I know you're not a bad kid."

"Thank you, sir."

"So long, Cary."

"Good-bye, sir."

The footsteps echoed against the walls as Mr. Grady walked away. The funny thing was, I didn't blame him. He'd done what he'd had to. Which was more than I could say for the rest, myself included.

I knew already what to expect from my father. On the phone all he had asked was "Why?" When he picked me up, it would be more of the same. How did it happen, Cary? How could you let it happen? Don't you know the difference between right and wrong? Didn't you know all along that it would explode in your face? He said I'd probably been punished enough. He just wanted me to explain it to him so that he and Mom could make some sense of it.

How was I supposed to explain that I wasn't so bright after all? How could I explain something I didn't understand? Not yet anyway.

I wasn't sure when it had started or how. It had something to do with all of us. Bobby and Joe and Billings, of course. Even Madison. And me. And being at Winslow, which sounds like a cop-out, only it isn't. Even though I couldn't blame the school for what had happened, I couldn't help feeling it would have been different someplace else.

That's not an excuse, just part of the explanation. To figure it all out, I would have to go back to the beginning, to the first day.

Chapter 2

Since it was founded the year after the Civil War ended, Winslow School has turned out six generations of boys who have gone on to distinguish themselves and the school in government, industry, science, and the arts. Two have won a Nobel Prize, eleven have served in the Senate or the House of Representatives, and one has been a Supreme Court justice. Two boys have become President of the United States.

—Winslow School catalog,
page 2

A week or so before summer ended one of the guys back home asked me why I had decided on Winslow School in the first place. I don't remember what I answered exactly, but the question stuck because I never imagined anyone asking. I'd be willing to bet a pair of Top-Siders that most Winslow boys would have been as surprised as I was.

The place is like a Preppie Hall of Fame. Becoming a Winslow boy sets you apart. It doesn't mean you're better than anyone else; it just means you have a better chance at everything. Which amounts to the same thing.

Right?

Wrong?

Maybe.

Anyway, I went.

1. Because Stanton Falls High isn't so hot academically or any other way.
2. Because even though I screw up on a lot of things, I seem to be some sort of genius when it comes to multiple choice.
3. Because my mother's great-aunt died last year and left money for my education. I only met her a couple of times, so it wasn't a big deal except for the money, which covers the ten thousand bucks a year it costs to house, feed, and educate your typical Winslow boy.

I'm not exactly sure what your typical Winslow boy is, but I have a feeling I'm not it. I'd elaborate on that here and now; but it would mean another list, and I'm trying to cut down on them. Lists are a sort of hobby of mine. My mother said they're more like an obsession; but she was only teasing, and besides, it isn't really true. I just happen to make up lists. Favorite friends, favorite teachers, best rock groups, that sort of thing. I've been doing it since I was eight, when I made up a list of something so dumb (even for an eight-year-old) that I'm never telling anyone what it was.

The only weird aspect of my list making is that I save them. I file them in alphabetical order in a cabinet in my room back home. It's not like I think they are going to insure my immortality or anything. It's just that I have a big chunk of my life on those scraps of paper. Throwing them out would have been like throwing away part of me.

The particular day in September when I first came to Winslow the lawns were lush and green from the rainy summer we'd been having and the leaves hadn't begun to turn. The quadrangle was filled with boys lugging their suitcases and stereos, ice skates and tennis rackets, and portable typewriters into the dorms. At Winslow the dorms are called houses.

Two trunks and a golf bag held the door to McKinley open. Inside, the air was stale from the house being closed all summer. The smell of ammonia rising from the linoleum hit me as I walked down the hall to my room. Our room, I mean. Mine and Ripley's and Katzenbach's. Although I hadn't said much more than hello to Ripley and hadn't even met Katzenbach, I knew their names. Before Labor Day the school had sent postcards informing new boys of their roommates' names and addresses. Theirs were the only names I was sure about.

I had no idea how the three of us were supposed to fit into McKinley No. 4. It was a small room for two people. For three, it was going to be a major challenge.

"Your folks leave already?"

Joe Ripley had the shortest crew cut I had ever seen. If he'd let his hair grow some, he probably would have been good-looking. He was well built, tall, and had very square features. His skin wasn't too good, though. He had acne. Nothing terminal. He'd outgrow it someday.

Before I went to Winslow, I'd never thought much about looks, not even my own. My brown hair is just long enough to part (a Princeton cut, the barber called it). In height and weight I am absolutely average and neither happy nor miserable about it. When I saw guys like Joe, though, I did feel kind of relieved not to have anything wrong with my skin.

While my mom and dad and I had been saying good-bye in the parking lot, Joe had taken matters into his own hands. He had arranged the single bed, a desk, a chair, and a bureau on one side of the room. The rest of the furniture, including the bunk beds, was crammed into the other half.

"I thought we were supposed to decide, all three of us, who was going to get what," I said.

"Katzenbach's late," Ripley said. "And I didn't know how long you were going to hang out with your folks. You don't mind, do you?"

I was stuck for an answer. If I admitted that I minded, which I did, Joe was going to think I was petty. If I said nothing, he would think I was a pushover. I remembered my father's saying it would take me awhile to adjust to living with the other boys.

"If it's okay with Katzenbach," I said, "it's okay with me." I hoped Joe would reconsider, but he didn't. He unfolded a pair of sheets and started to make up the single bed.

"If you guys don't like the bunks, we can change around next term," he said. "It's not my fault Katzenbach was supposed to be here hours ago."

He was right, of course. New boys were supposed to check in by noon, and it was almost three now.

"I don't know if it's fair to Katzenbach," I said.

"It's fair," Joe said. "Don't get into a sweat about it."

I pushed some of the furniture out of my way so I could make a path from the door to the bunk beds. My suitcases and footlocker were still in the hall, and I pushed them into the room. I rested the suitcases on the lower bunk. It was my way of claiming it for myself. If Joe was following the first-come, first-served philosophy, I had better do the same. At summer camp once I got the upper bunk and worried every night that I would roll over in my sleep and fall out of bed.

As I unpacked the new clothes my mother had sewn my name tags into, I tried to think up some friendly questions to ask Joe Ripley. So far the only things I knew about him were that he came from a small town in western Pennsylvania and that it had taken him twenty hours, including changes, on a Greyhound to get to Winslow. The few other boys who arrived without their parents had come from the airport in the Winslow School van. Also, Joe's luggage looked like it had seen better days. I didn't want to ask what his father did for a living. More than once my mother had told me that under no circumstances was I to ask that. It was like asking someone how much money they had. If someone wanted me to know, he'd tell me.

"You come from a big family?" I asked.

"Yeah," Joe said.

"How many brothers and sisters?"

"Three brothers, two sisters," he said.

"Older or younger?"

"Younger," Joe said. "All of them. How about you?"

"I'm an only child," I said.

"That's nice."

"That's kind of a funny thing to say," I said. "No one ever said that to me before."

"If there's only one kid, there's more to go around," he said. "You know what I mean."

Silently we both went about our unpacking. From the hall we heard the sounds of other boys dragging their things into the house. We heard them introducing themselves and asking each other where they were from. We heard them making little jokes and laughing too. But Joe and I said nothing. The others sounded like they were trying to be friends. Joe and I weren't even trying to be friendly. At least he wasn't. Back in Stanton Falls I had lots of friends, people I'd known practically all my life. The fact remained that I still wasn't very used to initiating new friendships. It sure looked like I was striking out with Joe Ripley.

Even if Joe had been first one there, he should have waited for Katzenbach to arrive before he took the best bed. If we'd picked straws or flipped a coin, he might still have ended up with the single bed anyway. Who was to know?

It was just that there was something about Joe Ripley that gave me the creeps. And though I wasn't going to take it too personally, I had a feeling Joe wasn't too crazy about me either.

Chapter 3

Situated on the banks of the Connecticut River
on the five hundred acres that served as the original site of the Winslow family's tobacco farms,
Winslow School boasts facilities that match those
of any other independent school in this country
as well as those of any number of smaller colleges. Thanks in large measure to the generosity
of our alumni, the handsome Georgian buildings
around the quadrangle which serve as the boys'
dormitories are complemented by a chapel, a library, two science centers, two gyms, a dining
hall, and a fully staffed infirmary.

—Winslow School catalog,
page 5

When Joe finished his unpacking, he looked at his
watch. "I got a meeting," he said.

"What's it for?" I asked.

"Bursary boys," he said. "You one of them?"

I shook my head.

"Didn't figure you would be," he said.

After Joe had left, I wished I had asked him what a
bursary boy was. Not asking questions when I didn't
understand something was one of my most common
failings. I was afraid to look dumb, especially here at
Winslow, where all the boys were so smart.

As far as I knew, there was nothing I was supposed

to do until supper. So I opened the Winslow catalog
to the page with the map on it and went exploring. I
was curious to know what was where. Plus it would
keep me from getting lost all the time my first couple
of days.

Like a lot of good ideas, mine wasn't an original
one. Other boys were wandering around the campus.
Most of them were in groups of twos and threes, but
I knew they were new boys, because they had their
catalogs with them too. I would have liked to join
someone, but I felt self-conscious introducing myself
to a group, even a small one, so I went it alone.

Not that I minded too much. I liked seeing the
campus through my own eyes and at my own pace. It
was beautiful. Great old trees everywhere. Immacu-
lately maintained lawns intersected by winding brick
paths. The buildings were mostly brick, too, with
white trim on the doors and windows and dark green
shutters. A brass plaque at the side of each entrance
indicated the donor. Some of the names, Rockefeller
and Vanderbilt, I recognized, but it was another, less
familiar name that stood out. The plaque at the library entrance explained that the annex was donated
by the Katzenbach Foundation.

As it turned out, I didn't need to know that my
roommate-to-be, Robert Katzenbach, was related to
the Katzenbach Foundation or that his father had reg-
istered him at Winslow the day he was born to know
that he was born to go to Winslow. The first time I
saw him I knew he belonged.

The limousine helped. Just as I was wandering
around the gates to the school, a black Lincoln came
to a stop in front of Main, the only building on the
entire Winslow campus without someone's name at

tached to it. A chauffeur in a black uniform got out and unloaded suitcases and shopping bags from the trunk. I tried to get a look at who was inside, but the tinted windows blocked my view. A moment later a boy a little shorter than I was stepped out. His curly blond hair was almost white from the summer sun, and he had a great tan. He was a little overweight, but he wasn't fat. Everything about him was very round. He was wearing a T-shirt, cutoff jeans, dirty sneakers, and no socks.

It wasn't until the chauffeur got back into the Lincoln and pulled away that the boy noticed me.

"You the welcoming committee?" he asked.

"You a new boy?" I asked back. Although I was wearing the blue blazer and the tie which the school required, I was feeling a little intimidated by the boy's clothes and manner.

"Surprised?" he asked. He looked pleased.

"New boys were supposed to be here before lunch," I said.

"I figured lunch was for the benefit of the parents mostly," he said. "My brother says no one ever ruined his health by skipping a meal around here. How awful was it?"

"Not good," I said. "My name's Cary Carmichael. I'm a new boy too."

"I'm Katzenbach," he said.

"Robert Katzenbach?"

"Or Bobby," he said. "How'd you know?"

"We're roommates."

"You know that for sure?" He looked at me with considerably more interest now.

"It was on the postcard they sent at the end of the summer," I said.

"We were still in France," he said. "Sometimes the maid forgets to forward the mail." He held out his hand, and we shook. "It looks like the rest of the welcoming committee has called it quits for the day. You lead the way, Carmichael."

It always made me uncomfortable being called by my last name, but I figured at Winslow I'd better get used to it. I picked up the shopping bags, all four of them, while Bobby picked up the suitcases.

In the five minutes it took us to get to the McKinley steps I knew more about Bobby Katzenbach than I had found out about Joe Ripley in two hours. Bobby's family had a duplex on Park Avenue in New York, and they had spent the last three summers in France because they were tired of Long Island, where they had a house they used for weekends the rest of the year. All his life he had gone to private schools. In New York, he said, no one went to public schools. He also said he had a brother who had gone on to Princeton after he had graduated from Winslow two years before.

I told Bobby that I had grown up in a small town a hundred miles west of Winslow and that my father taught French at the college there. Bobby had heard of Stanton College because a cousin of his had gone there after flunking out of Dartmouth. Stanton College wasn't Ivy League, but it wasn't a flunk-out school either. I wasn't sure Bobby was knocking the college, so I didn't say anything.

I told him about Joe Ripley.

"It's not a double?" he asked. "When my brother was here, all the rooms were doubles. Even for the new boys."

"The room *is* a double," I said. "It's just that there are three of us in it."

"What's Ripley like?"

"He doesn't talk much," I said.

"But he hasn't got elephant breath or anything, does he?"

"Just a sort of hamburger face," I said.

"What's that mean?"

"You know, acne."

Bobby laughed. "A hamburger face you call it?"

"It's not funny," I said. "Wait till you see it."

"I never heard 'hamburger face,'" Bobby said. "I think it's hilarious." He giggled more than the expression deserved.

"Don't mention it," I said. "Especially to Joe." Bobby's laughing made me feel anxious. I didn't want something like that to get back to Joe.

When Bobby and I got to No. 4, Joe was back from his meeting. He was lying on his bed reading a paperback.

"I see what you mean," Bobby said as he surveyed the room. I hoped he wasn't talking about Joe's acne. "Hi, there," he said to Joe. "I guess the early birds got the worms around here. Would it make any difference to you guys if I told you heights give me severe nosebleeds?"

"Do you have a note from your doctor?" Joe asked.

I smiled. Maybe it took Bobby to bring out Joe's sense of humor.

"Where you from?" Bobby dropped his suitcases in the narrow path that led to the bunk beds.

"Pennsylvania," Joe said.

"Whereabouts?"

"The western part. You never heard of the town."

"Coal mines there, aren't there?" Bobby asked. "Is your family in coal?"

"My grandfather worked in the mines," Joe said.

"What's your dad do?" Bobby asked. Apparently his mother and mine read different etiquette books.

"He has a pharmacy," Joe said.

"I guess your family's moving up in the world," Bobby said.

Bobby laughed, and so did I. Joe didn't.

"Is that supposed to be a joke?" he asked.

"Sorry," Bobby said. "You're not sensitive about that sort of thing, are you?"

Joe didn't answer.

Bobby emptied the shopping bags. A mass of crumpled shirts and jeans lay on the floor. "If there's anything you guys want to know about me, go ahead and ask. I've got nothing to hide."

"How long are you planning on leaving that crud on the floor?" Joe asked.

"That stuff ain't crud," Bobby said. "It's my fall wardrobe. Either of you see a laundry list around here?"

Laundry lists were just about the only kind of list I've never made up, but I tore the top sheet off a pad on one of the bureaus and handed it to him.

"I've got nothing to hide either," Joe said.

Bobby looked up from the list he was making. "Huh?"

"I didn't want you to get the impression that I'm ashamed of anything," Joe said, "because I'm not."

I guessed I was wrong about Bobby's bringing out Joe's sense of humor. Joe was offended. Maybe should have apologized for laughing, but I didn't.

"I didn't mean you were ashamed," Bobby said. "If I said something to make you sore, I'm sorry."

"Are you the Katzenbach Annex?" Joe asked.

"That's my father's old man," Bobby said. "I'm just the grandson of the annex."

"What's your father do?"

"He's kind of a stockbroker."

"He invests other people's money?"

"He invests his own," Bobby said.

"Is that a full-time job?"

"It keeps him busy," Bobby said.

Bobby stuffed his clothes into a pair of laundry bags and tossed them against the wall.

"How come you brought dirty clothes?" Joe asked.

"What makes you think they're dirty?" Bobby asked. "I just got tired of packing things in suitcases. It was easier this way."

"I guess it's okay if you don't have to work for your money," Joe said.

"I'm too young to work," Bobby said. "What difference does it make anyway? It's just some laundry."

I knew what Bobby and Joe were talking about, but I didn't know how to explain it to either of them.

There was a knock on the door. A tall boy with red hair and so many freckles that they looked like a tan stood in the doorway.

"Carmichael," he read from a list. "Katzenbach and Ripley. You them?"

The three of us nodded.

"I'm Kevin Ludlow," he said. "I'm your counselor."

"You're on the faculty?" Joe asked.

Kevin smiled. "I'm a senior. I live next door. I'm supposed to keep you guys in line this year. Next

year you're someone else's problem. Till then I'm
here to help you find your way around. Anytime you
have a problem knock on my door. I was a new boy
once."

I liked Kevin Ludlow. He sounded like he meant
the knock-on-my-door-if-you-have-a-problem stuff.

"Which one of you is Katzenbach?"

Bobby stepped forward.

"You missed lunch. How come?"

"I didn't miss much, did I?"

"You were supposed to be here. What's your excuse?"

"I guess I don't have one," Bobby said.

"That could get you in trouble," Kevin said.

"I can come up with one," Bobby said. "My chauffeur took the wrong exit on the Connecticut Turn-
pike. How's that?"

"Sounds like you were better off with no excuse,"
Joe said. "Who's going to believe you have your own
private chauffeur?"

Bobby shrugged. "I may need you for a witness,
Carmichael," he said. "Sorry to impose on such brief
acquaintance."

"Supper's in half an hour," Kevin said. "The Head
will speak, and I'll give you guys the grand tour tomorrow. Okay?"

The three of us nodded.

"Oh, and put on some decent clothes, Katzenbach,"
Kevin said. "Jacket and tie."

"The whole bit?"

"Yeah," Kevin said.

"If you don't have a jacket, you can borrow from
me," Joe said. "I've got extras."

I guessed that Joe was making a joke. At least he
was laughing.

Chapter 4

Hail we the Founding Fathers
As we march through glade and glen.
Pale youth on the brink of tomorrow
Are tomorrow's Winslow men.

—Final chorus of "O Winslow"

The dining hall was the largest room at Winslow. Its dark paneled walls were three stories high and spanned the width of the quadrangle. The windows extended almost to the ceiling, and a fireplace, twenty feet or so across and ten feet high, dominated one side. Thirty-five tables, which sat twelve people each, were placed neatly in rows.

That night the new boys sat at the tables at one end of the hall. The old boys occupied the rest of the tables. The next day we would receive our official seating assignments for the term, and the new boys would be integrated with the old boys.

Bobby and I sat next to each other. Joe sat at the same table but at the other side. The rest of the chairs were filled by other boys from McKinley. I recognized some of their faces and learned some of their names, too: Walsh and Voorhies, who had the room across the hall; Stearns, from the end of the hall.

Before supper the Headmaster, Mr. Walton Kretch, welcomed us to the school, and the chaplain, Mr. Hugh Webster, prayed for us, our school, and our country in a grace that lasted almost five minutes. During the meal we were serenaded by the Winslow Warblers, who sang a medley of Winslow songs. At the end they sang the school hymn. The faculty and the boys rose. The Headmaster wiped a tear from his face. Even though I had been a Winslow boy less than a day, I was moved too.

Somberly we filed out of the dining hall and returned to our rooms. As we got ready for bed, few of us spoke. No one, it seemed, wanted to shatter the spell. In the morning I was surprised that I had slept so soundly in a strange place.

The spell of the night, however, disappeared. With only one day left before classes began, the new boys were rushed through orientation meetings, meetings with our advisers, trips to the school store, and tours of the campus. Presidents of the various student clubs held meetings in the common rooms of the houses and invited us to apply for membership. The Winslow Dramat sounded interesting. Maybe I would try out for it. The director of the athletics program outlined the intramural sports scene. Fall tennis sounded the best to me.

At the end of the afternoon Kevin stopped by our room with our schedules. By and large, the new boys took the same courses: English I, History I, Algebra I, Latin I, and first-year French, German, Spanish, Russian, or Italian. Joe was enrolled in German I, Bobby in Spanish I, and I was in French III.

Since the summer I had known that I would be in third-year French. Bobby and Joe were impressed. I explained that my father was a professor of French and had been tutoring me for the last three years. For some reason Bobby was less impressed than before.

Was it because he wasn't impressed with Stanton College? I wondered.

Joe, on the other hand, was more impressed even though he had never heard of Stanton College. He asked Bobby why he was taking Spanish when he had spent the last two summers in France. Bobby grinned and shrugged, but I knew Joe had him pegged now. Bobby had gone from rich-boy type to stupid rich-boy type. Spanish was a gut course everywhere, I guessed.

We filed up for our dining hall assignments. Joe and I were the only new boys at Mr. Grady's table. Mr. Grady, it turned out, knew who I was before I knew who he was.

"*Ça va, Monsieur Carmichael?*" he asked when we all were seated.

"*Bien, monsieur,*" I said.

"*Vous êtes dans ma classe, n'est-ce pas?*"

"Yes," I said. "*Oui, je veux dire. La troisième.*"

Even if Joe was impressed, I knew speaking French wasn't going to win me any points with the other boys. Regular guys don't show off their foreign languages, even at Winslow.

When the meal was over, Joe and I were walking back to McKinley together. I had remembered the name of only one other boy at the table. His name was Billings. Joe said he was president of the Student Council.

"What's a bursary boy?" I asked.

"It's a euphemism for scholarship boy," he said matter-of-factly.

"What do they need a euphemism for?"

"They don't," he said. "They just think they do. Not having a lot of money is embarrassing for some people, so they dress it up and it makes everyone feel a whole lot better."

"But you shouldn't be embarrassed," I said. "It's not your fault your parents aren't rich."

"It's not even my parents' fault," he said.

"I didn't say that," I said, feeling that Joe had twisted the meaning. "I meant it's nothing for you to feel embarrassed about. My folks aren't rich either."

"But you don't need a scholarship, do you?"

I shook my head. I had a feeling that it was no time to mention Great-Aunt Dorothy and the inheritance.

"There are a lot of people who have money they didn't earn and probably didn't deserve," Joe said. "They're the ones who make up the euphemisms, Cary. It's like when Katzenbach says I have something to hide because my old man has a pharmacy and my old man's old man was a coal miner. He thinks being poor is something I'd just as soon sweep under the carpet or something."

"That's not what Bobby said," I said.

"If you think about it, you'll see that's what he meant."

"What did they do at the meeting?" I asked, not sure I did see.

"What they did was to hand out these dinky jobs. Like I've got to spend an hour each day at the Xerox copier in the faculty lounge. They even gave me my very own key. It's supposed to make me feel like I'm earning my keep."

"Does it make you angry at the school?"

"Heck, no," Joe said. "I'm glad to be here. Maybe I'm even grateful. Kids from my neck of the woods don't get too many chances. This place could be the big one for me."

"So you can do what?" I asked.

"So I can get out of my neck of the woods, of course."

I was beginning to understand why Joe frightened me. He was so determined that he didn't seem like any kid I had ever met. I should have admired him, I suppose, but I thought you had to like someone before you looked up to him.

The first assignment we got in our first class was to make up a list. It was Mr. Martin's English class, which happened to be the only class Joe and Bobby and I shared. Bobby and I were sitting together, and just before the bell rang, Joe came in and took a seat on the other side of the room. I wondered if he was avoiding us. Or just Bobby. Or just me.

When the bell rang, Mr. Martin came in. He wore jeans and he had a beard. He put his jacket on the back of his chair and loosened his tie.

"We're going to start with character," he said. "It's the core of any story. It's what makes the story work."

On his desk were a dozen copies of *The Catcher in the Rye*. I hadn't read it, but I knew it was about a boy who goes to prep school. Mr. Martin distributed the copies.

"It may add to your enjoyment if I tell you the book has been banned from some public schools around the country," he said.

"It is dirty?" Schumacher asked. He lived across the hall from us. He was the first kid in the class to have a nickname: Mole. He was the shortest kid at Winslow, and he moved very slowly.

"Some people like to think it is," Mr. Martin said.

"If you're a prude, Schumacher, I'll try to find you an expurgated edition."

The class laughed, and Schumacher turned several shades of red. Right away I could tell that Mr. Martin was going to be everyone's favorite teacher. Probably even Schumacher's.

"As you read it, I want you to describe for me what Holden Caulfield's character is," he said. "And I want you to describe it in terms of what he wants. I'd also like you to make up a list in which you describe yourselves in terms of what you want. You may even learn something about yourselves."

Mr. Martin went on about Holden Caulfield and *The Catcher in the Rye*, but I was already trying to make up a list in my head. I didn't get very far on my own, so I started on Joe's and Bobby's.

Already I knew what Joe wanted. It was to get away from his hometown. I guessed he wanted to be really rich.

For Bobby's list I wasn't sure. He was already rich. Maybe he wanted to be richer, but I didn't think so. Bobby liked putting on a show. Did he do it to make people like him? I didn't think so. He certainly hadn't done anything so far to make either Joe or me like him. He just wanted to impress us.

Getting to be liked was more important to me than I wanted to admit, and it wasn't something I would have put on the class assignment. If I'd been back home, I might have written it on a secret list and hidden it in the cabinet in my room. The trouble with Winslow was, there weren't any good hiding places.

Chapter 5

Two hundred yards east of the quadrangle is the
Vanderbeck Gymnasium, and a hundred yards
beyond is the Whitney Gymnasium. In addition
to four basketball courts, the gyms contain two
swimming pools, a half-dozen squash courts, two
indoor tennis courts, and a rifle range. For out-
door sports there are three hockey rinks, more
tennis courts, baseball diamonds, and fields for
football, soccer, lacrosse, and track. It is a founding precept of the school that lessons learned on
the sports field are as necessary to a Winslow
boy's development as the lessons learned in the
classroom.

—Winslow School catalog,
page 7

The wake-up bell rang at six-thirty. The next one
went off five minutes later. Get up. Take a shower.
Get dressed. The seven o'clock bell was breakfast,
cafeteria-style, no assigned tables. The next bell
sounded at seven-thirty. Make your bed, clean up
your room, and wait for inspection.

Eight was chapel. The new boys sat in the balcony.
Mr. Grady sat at one side and played the organ. The
rest of the masters and boys sat on the main floor.
From eight twenty-five to one there were classes. Old
boys went back to their rooms when they had free

periods. New boys reported to the study hall on the second floor of Main. One o'clock was lunch. Two o'clock was the last class of the day. Three to five was sports. Five-thirty to six-fifteen was more study hall for the new boys. Dinner was at six-thirty. Evening study hall lasted from seven-thirty to nine-twenty. Lights-out was at ten.

In the fifteen and a half waking hours there were in a Winslow day, the school granted eighty-five minutes of independence. If I skipped my morning shower, I could stretch it into an hour and a half.

Which was why it wasn't until the end of the day that Bobby and I had a chance to say anything more than hello to each other.

"What are you doing about sports?" he asked me when he and I were walking around the quadrangle after the nine-twenty bell.

"What are we supposed to do?" I asked.

"We've got to do a sport," he said. "Everybody does. Which one are we going to pick?"

"We have to play the same sport?"

"I don't see why not," he said. "We're both Winslow Blues, so why not do the same sport?"

"What's a Blue?" I asked.

"It's one of the intramural teams," Bobby said. "There's the Reds and the Greens, and you and I are Blues."

"How come you know we're Blues and I don't?" I asked.

"Because I went down to the Vanderbeck Gym this afternoon and checked the lists. Ripley's a Green, in case you're interested. Anyway, we all have to decide by tomorrow afternoon. What's it going to be?"

"What are they offering?"

"Well, there's football," Bobby said. "Good sport but a dumb idea unless you're planning on becoming a superjock."

"What makes you think I'm not?"

"Ever look in a mirror, Carmichael?" he asked. "If you go out for football, proceed at your own risk. As for myself, I'm sticking to something a little less dangerous. A neck brace would stretch out all my crew-neck sweaters."

"You've talked me out of football," I said. "What else have they got around here?"

"Not a whole lot," Bobby said. "There's soccer. And there's track. And there's fall tennis."

"I'll go out for fall tennis," I said. "That's what I've been planning on anyway."

"Wait until the spring," Bobby said. "Spring tennis is supposed to be okay."

"Explain, Bobby."

"Fall tennis is definitely for losers," he said. "You don't want to ruin your reputation before you get one, do you?"

"I don't know what I'd do without you," I said.

"That's what I'm here for," Bobby said. "Track's out too."

"Uncos and spazes?"

"Worse," Bobby said. "My brother says the track people are a little weird. They're not keen on getting along with other people. It's not a contact sport, so I guess it figures."

"Football players who break each other's neck do get along? Is that what you mean?"

"That's the general idea, Carmichael," he said. "Look, if you don't want my expert opinions, I'm not going to force them on you."

"Don't think I'm not grateful, Bobby," I said. "Let's see. Football's out. Track is out. Tennis is out. So what's left?"

"I wondered how long it was going to take you to get to the point," he said. "We're going out for soccer in case you're still interested."

"I never played soccer before," I said.

"Me either," he said. "But it'll be good for your image. I promise."

So the next day, after our last class, Bobby and I went out for soccer. In the gym we found our lockers and changed into our official Winslow Blue T-shirts and sneakers. As I waited for Bobby, I repeated the locker combination over and over to myself. Already I was trying to minimize the risks of the sporting life at Winslow.

In back of the gym boys from all the classes were grouped together according to their colors. Bobby and I headed for the Blues. Just as we got there, a great cheer of "Yay, Blue" resounded in the air. A moment later there was a "Yay, Green" and then a "Yay, Red." All of a sudden boys were running in a dozen different directions.

"What are we supposed to do now?" I asked.

"Ask someone, I guess," Bobby said.

"See anyone you recognize?"

"Everyone I know is a Red or a Green," Bobby said.

"Sorry I asked," I said, not believing that Bobby knew any more boys at Winslow than I did.

Coming toward us was Kevin Ludlow, walking by himself.

"You guys lost?" he asked.

"Not yet, but we're getting there," I said.

"Do you know where we're supposed to go?" Bobby asked.

"What sport are you going out for?" Kevin asked.

"We're soccer," Bobby said.

"I'm going in the same direction," Kevin said.

"You play soccer?" Bobby asked.

"Yeah."

"What position?"

"Center," Kevin said. He pointed to a man standing in the next field, where twenty-five other boys in blue T-shirts were assembled. "That's Mr. Grummond. He's the coach for the Blue intramurals. Go over and introduce yourselves. He'll tell you what you're supposed to do."

"Aren't you coming?"

"I'm over there," Kevin said, gesturing toward another field where a group of older boys were kicking a soccer ball around.

"What going on over there?" Bobby asked.

"First team," Kevin said.

"Did you know my brother, Peter, when he was here?" Bobby asked.

"Attaway Katzenbach is your brother?"

Bobby nodded.

"They called your brother Attaway?" I asked.

"He was captain of the varsity soccer team," Bobby said.

"And the fastest thing they ever saw around here," Kevin said. "That's how he got his nickname. How's he doing?"

"Captain of the Princeton jayvees," Bobby said.

So now I knew why Bobby was going out for soccer even though he had never played before. It also

explained why he had made such a point of talking
me into it.

Bobby and I walked toward Mr. Grummond. He
was in his thirties, but his hair was going gray at the
temples.

"Katzenbach and Carmichael reporting for duty,
sir," Bobby said. "He's Carmichael. I'm Katzenbach."

"I know who you are, Katzenbach," Mr. Grummond said sourly. "I know who your brother is, too,
but you're still late."

"Had a little trouble finding the place," Bobby
said.

"More trouble than the other boys," Mr. Grummond said. He looked over the other Blues to prove
his point.

Bobby and I sat down on the grass.

"Okay," Grummond said. "How many of you
know the soccer rules?"

The boys around me, Bobby included, raised their
hands.

"I thought you never played," I whispered.

"Shut up and fake it, Carmichael, before you make
a fool of yourself."

I raised my hand too.

"How many of you ever played the game before?"

We all raised our hands.

"Then I'll divide you into groups and you can kick
the ball around awhile. Tomorrow I'll make up the A,
B, and C teams. If any of you show real promise, you
can try out for the junior varsity."

Mr. Grummond directed Bobby and me to follow
one group of boys down the field. He tossed a ball to
one of the older boys and dropped it to the ground.

The boy kicked the ball to the boy standing next to him.

As far as I could tell, no one seemed to be playing any particular position, so Bobby and I followed the others as the ball was kicked toward the other end of the field. A boy kicked the ball into the goal. Another boy kicked it back to our end. We followed the ball some more, but Bobby and I stuck to one side of the field. So far the ball hadn't rolled there. If our luck held, it wouldn't come near us until Bobby and I had figured out what we were supposed to do next.

Back and forth, up and down the field. We continued to follow the ball at a safe distance, though I was getting winded. But not as badly as Bobby. I could hear him breathing heavily. Was anyone keeping score? Five to two, I thought. Theirs.

A boy made a wild kick. The ball came toward Bobby and me. I tried to kick the ball back to the center, but it bounced off the side of Bobby's sneaker before I could get to it. The ball rolled to a halt a few feet from us. Bobby tapped it with the toe of his sneaker. It rolled another few feet. No one was running toward us, so it was still ours. Bobby kicked it, and then I kicked it. We were running again, alternating our kicks as best we could.

When we got toward the end of the field, we kicked the ball to the center. No one was playing goalie, and still none of the other boys was close behind us. I kicked the ball to Bobby. Before it reached him, I realized what we'd been doing and why no one was trying to intercept us. I heard our teammates yelling at us. I raced to Bobby, trying to kick the ball away before he got to it.

I was too late. With one sure kick Bobby kicked the

ball into the goal. He turned to me and grinned. The screaming turned to laughter. Bobby understood without my saying anything. He looked stricken.

"Asshole," he said. "Asshole, asshole."

The scrimmage went on. Our side made three more goals with no more help from Bobby or me. The final score was six to five. Bobby had scored the winning goal.

For the other side.

The next day Grummond assigned us both to the C team.

Chapter 6

September 28

Dear Mom and Dad,

I think I'm adjusting. I passed my first French quiz (92) and I'm getting along okay with my roommates, the rich one especially. We're both on the C team in soccer, but it's okay. Someone has to start at the bottom.

Love,
Cary

P.S.: Tell Mr. Freed at the bank that Aunt Dorothy's getting her money's worth.

Bobby had been assigned to Mr. Leonard's table at the center of the dining hall. He made it clear he wasn't very happy about it.

"Is Leonard a dip?" I asked.

"He's okay," Bobby said. "You know Wallingford?"

"The junior who's going bald?"

"The one with the scar in the side of his face where his mouth should be," Bobby said.

"What's the scar say?"

"Calls me Wrong Way Katzenbach," Bobby said. "I'm ruined before I begin."

"You could drop the soccer for something else," I suggested.

"I tried to go out for tennis," he said. "Grummond wouldn't allow it."

"You shouldn't take it so hard," I said. "We both were running in the wrong direction."

"It's not the same," Bobby said. "You didn't make the goal. You don't have an older brother you'll never live up to."

"Don't make a big deal out of it," I said. "It'll pass."

"Maybe," Bobby said uncertainly. Both of us knew that nicknames had a way of sticking. "I'd give anything if I could get out of soccer and out of Leonard's table too. You guys really lucked out with Grady."

"Grady's okay," I said. "He's not so hot."

"Billings and Madison are," Bobby said. "They're the kings of the hill around here. They don't waste their time picking on lowly frosh."

As far as I was concerned Bobby was only half right. After a week at Mr. Grady's table I still didn't see what was so hot about Madison. Billings, though, was something else again.

Of course, he was president of the Student Council, but it was more than that. It was more than being tall, dark, and handsome, too, although Billings was all three. He had what my folks called presence. If he was in a crowd, he would be the first person you noticed. He was the one you kept your eyes on. Without raising his voice, without trying at all, he dominated the table.

Especially on Thursday evenings, when Mr. Grady skipped dinner and went to the Philharmonic in Springfield.

The bell rang, and the boys sat down in their usual seats. Except for Billings, who took Mr. Grady's seat. After the Head had said grace, there was a scramble by the waiters for the swinging doors that led to the kitchen. Rogers, our waiter, placed a casserole in front of Billings.

"I'll do the honors," Billings said. "Unless one of you gentlemen has an objection."

No one did, of course. Billings cast an eye over the food. "What epicurean delights has cook whipped up for us tonight?" he asked. "Aha! Elephant scabs. What a treat!"

He picked up a spoon and began to serve. He handed the first plate to me, and I passed it along. Elephant scabs were breaded veal cutlets. Even though the name was enough to turn your stomach, the boys laughed.

"So how did we do on our French quiz today?" Billings asked me as he dished out more scabs.

"Ninety-three," I said.

"Very respectable, Mr. Carmichael," he said. He was imitating Mr. Grady. I didn't ask him how he had done on the quiz because I had seen his grade when Grady was handing back the tests. Billings had got a 78. At Winslow 78s were not respectable. I wondered if it was because of his weak French grades that Billings was withdrawn in class. Certainly he wasn't like that anywhere else.

Madison sat on the other side of Billings. He was okay-looking, but pale, almost anemic. Most of the time he looked bored or irritated. I couldn't tell which. Nor could I tell why Bobby thought he was so hot. But Madison was always hanging out with Billings, so maybe it was just the reflected glory.

"You'd better make sure that Billings isn't looking over your shoulder during exams," Madison said. "You still stink at French, don't you, Billings?"

"It's not charming of you to mention my French

grades," Billings said. "Especially when there are people eating."

"How come they moved you up to French Three?" Madison asked.

"Carmichael's father is a French professor," Billings said, answering for me. "Which makes Carmichael here a ringer."

"Ever meet any French girls?" Madison asked.

I was about to explain that I hadn't ever been to France when Billings interrupted.

"Please, Madison," he said, "can't you see you're embarrassing the lad?"

"My uncle got clap from a French whore once," Madison said. "When he was in the army."

"I *am* impressed," Billings said. "Should we have a moment of silence for your poor uncle?"

"Did your uncle die?" I asked.

The other boys laughed. I recoiled. Somehow I had a definite knack for humiliating myself whenever the talk got around to sex.

"You die from syphilis sometimes," Joe said to me. "Clap you just get sick from." He was sitting on the other side of me, and he was speaking just loud enough for me to hear, both of which I was grateful for.

Billings and Madison went back to their elephant scabs. I reached for the aluminum pitcher. It was empty.

I pushed back my chair. Before I stood up, Billings put his hand on my forearm.

"Who killed the milk?" he asked the table.

There was no response.

"Denny, you killed the cow, didn't you?"

"Not me," Denny said.

"Would you mind telling me who did, then?"

"I wasn't looking," Denny said.

"I was," Billings said. "You get us some more milk. Don't stick Carmichael with the trip to the kitchen."

I released my grip on the pitcher. Denny went to the kitchen with it. Billings picked up his fork. When Denny came back with the pitcher, I poured myself a glass even though I wasn't thirsty anymore.

Billings put his knife and fork on his plate and pushed the plate away from him. It was time for Rogers to clear.

"No stacking at the table," Billings reminded him. "Just because Grady isn't here doesn't mean we have to let go of all decorum."

Dessert was a large bowl of canned peaches topped with a thick layer of whipped cream.

"Remember what this horror is called, Carmichael?" Billings asked me as he picked up the serving spoon and dumped the cream and peaches onto plates.

"Beethoven's Last Movement?" I asked.

"Very good, Mr. Carmichael," Billings said.

"Very gross, Mr. Carmichael," Madison said.

"That's a compliment. Madison is the master of the gross-out. You should have seen him last year over at Bancroft."

"I beg your pardon," Madison said.

"I was referring to your pursuit of Wendy Morrison, the belle at our sister school," Billings said. "A total gross-out. And that's not a compliment."

"Come on, Billings," Madison said. "I was at my most charming."

"Morrison didn't think so," Billings said. "She was totally grossed out, old boy."

"That's her upbringing," Madison said. "Morrison's too bourgeois."

"What's bourgeois?" Joe asked.

"Ask your roomie here," Madison said. "It comes from the French."

"It means middle-class," I said.

"What's that got to do with anything?" Joe asked.

"Middle-class girls don't put out," Madison explained.

"Not for that stupid line of yours," Billings said.

"It's worked before," Madison said. "It'll work again. I'll probably score with it at the pig pool next month."

"I'm shocked," Billings said. "Is that how you refer to those splendid mixers we have every now and then with Bancroft? Crude, Madison. Very, very crude. Don't listen to a word he says, Carmichael."

Billings put his hands over my ears. Everyone at the table roared with laughter, me included.

"What's the line you use?" Denny asked.

"Oh, boys, it's a trade secret," Madison said.

"But Billings knows."

"I told him more out of pity than anything else."

"Screw you, chum," Billings said good-naturedly. He took his hands away from my ears.

"Honest, if word gets out, no women over twelve and a half will be safe," Madison said.

"Out of pity, you should tell the rest of us," Denny pleaded.

"Don't, Denny," Madison said. "Think of the civil disorder that would result throughout western Massachusetts."

"We're not leaving the table till you tell," Rogers said.

"Well, okay," Madison said. "I know when I'm trapped. What you do is wait till she's having a little trouble catching her breath. You hold her real close. You nibble on her ear and whisper into it, 'Lie down. I think I love you.'"

"Crude," Billings said. "Don't listen to him, boys. Sex is a beautiful experience, just the way they tell you in physical hygiene."

All the boys were whooping and laughing and pounding the table so hard that the boys and masters at the other tables were beginning to stare at us.

The bell rang and everyone stood. Billings put his hand on my shoulder.

"No one ever scores at the mixers," he said. "Madison says anything to get a laugh, okay?"

I nodded, more grateful than I would have wanted him to know. Billings was just all-around terrific, and he made me feel terrific too. Like they say, reflected glory's better than no glory at all.

Chapter 7

                                          October 4

Dear Mom and Dad,

Thanks for the prep school handbook. It's not
so that the boys put adhesive tape around their
loafers, but everything else is true, I guess. Sorry
it looked like I was putting a price tag on the
value of education. I didn't mean to, but sometimes this place makes you dwell on that sort of
stuff. Some of the kids (like Bobby) are so incred-
ibly rich, and some of the others are really poor.
Like Joe.

I'll let you know if a class war breaks out.

                    Love,
                    Cary

A week later the bad stuff between Joe and Bobby
started for real. Since the first day they had hardly
spoken. When they did speak, it was mostly barbs,
dumb things I usually didn't get. They seemed to be
developing a secret language to get at each other
with.

It was the day the boxes arrived from Bloom-
ingdale's in New York. In one carton were three yel-
low bedspreads. In the other were curtains to match.

It was before evening study, and Bobby and I were
looking them over when Joe came in. It was getting

cooler now, the second week of October. Joe tossed his Windbreaker on his bed.

"I don't want a bedspread, thanks," Joe said. "You guys do what you like with the curtains."

"You don't like them?" Bobby asked.

"I don't need a bedspread, that's all," Joe said.

"There's going to be one brokenhearted mother running around New York," Bobby said. "And all thanks to you too. I don't know how you're going to live with the guilt, Ripley."

"Don't worry about it," Joe said. "If I can live with you, I can live with anything."

Bobby turned to me. "My mother could exchange them," he said. "Maybe she could get something in polyester."

It was a Bobby kind of crack, right up there with "Hard day in the Xerox room, Ripley?"

"If you want me to pay for the bedspread, I will," Joe said. "I just don't want it on my bed."

"I wouldn't expect you to pay for something you don't want," Bobby said. "Besides, it was supposed to be a present."

"And I'm looking a gift horse in the mouth?" Joe asked.

"It doesn't matter," Bobby said. "I just want the room to look nice."

"It's going to take more than some curtains and some bedspreads to pull that off," Joe said.

Joe retreated behind his earphones while Bobby and I looked around the room. Even though the three of us kept it pretty tidy, it was still cramped and crummy. All the furniture was falling apart, and the paint was beginning to peel. It was funny, but the school looked a whole lot nicer on the outside than i did on the inside. The school's benefactors liked to have their donations seen.

"Maybe your mother could send up an interior decorator from New York," Joe said. He still had his earphones on, so there wasn't much point in saying anything back. Even Bobby could see that.

In spite of his casual arrival at Winslow, it turned out that Bobby was fastidious about his things. His sweaters were folded meticulously in plastic bags. His bed was made so neatly you could bounce a dime on it. When he came back from class, he didn't hurl his books in the general direction of his bed the way Joe and I did. Instead, he emptied his book bag, book by book, and placed them in alphabetical order on the top shelf of the bookcase on his desk.

On the bottom shelf were his photographs. The largest one, like the others, was in a silver frame. In the photo Bobby and his brother were throwing an inflated beach ball around at their house on Long Island. In the background was the Katzenbachs' summer house, the one they didn't spend the summers at. It was a rambling, shingled building with white shutters and a porch that wrapped around three sides. Bobby was wearing a pair of cutoff jeans. His brother was wearing a bathing suit and a Winslow sweatshirt with a varsity *W* on it.

The other photos were what they called studio portraits: one of his brother; another of his mother sitting in a wing chair with his father standing behind her. Bobby's parents were good-looking. Young-looking too.

Sometimes during the evening study hours Bobby would pick up one of the photos, blow away some of the dust, and linger over it before he put it back on the bookshelf. It was the only time I wondered if he was homesick. I was pretty sure he was.

Joe had only one photograph, and he kept it on the top of his bureau. It was in color, and it showed a girl leaning against the side of a truck. The photo was overexposed, so you couldn't tell if the girl was pretty, but she did have a lot of blond hair.

I didn't have any photos. I figured the less I had to remind me of home, the less homesick I would get.

"I'm going to put the Princeton banner on the wall over my bed," Bobby said. "I hope you guys don't mind."

"You've already decided you're going there?" I asked.

"Maybe," Bobby said. "I don't know. If I get in."

He hoisted himself to the upper bunk. "Hand me the thumbtacks on my desk, will you, Carmichael?"

He held the banner against the wall and tacked it up. "Is it even?" he asked.

"Higher on the right," Joe said. "You should tack it into the molding."

Bobby leaned back to have a look. If he had heard Joe, he was pretending he hadn't. Joe's earphones drove him crazy. Joe could talk, but no one could talk back to him.

"Joe's right," I said. "It's a little high on the right."

Bobby tacked the banner into the molding. Without looking back at it, he jumped from the upper bunk to the floor. He turned on the gooseneck lamp on his desk and sat down.

The seven-thirty bell went off. I sat down at my desk and opened my Caesar. For the next hour and fifty minutes we were supposed to have complete silence.

Kevin did his seven-thirty inspection. The door to the room was open, but he knocked anyway.

"Everybody at the books?" he asked.

I turned to him and held up my Caesar. Bobby was staring at his photographs.

"Katzenbach," Kevin said, "you're supposed to be studying the books, not the pictures of your family."

"I'm memorizing stuff," Bobby said.

Kevin peered over Bobby's shoulder. "What are you memorizing?"

" 'Ozymandias.' "

"Why don't you have your poetry reader in front of you?" Kevin asked. "It'd make the memorizing easier."

"I like it this way," Bobby said. "It's the way I always memorize things."

"Just trying to help," Kevin said. "Don't get upset."

"I'm not upset," Bobby said. "Just don't pick on me, okay?"

Kevin raised his eyebrows. Why Bobby thought Kevin was picking on him was beyond me.

Joe was lying on his bed. On his lap was a copy of a paperback book. Maybe it was *The Catcher in the Rye*, but I didn't think so. His earphones were pulled down around his neck.

"You'd better get to your desk, Ripley," Kevin said.

"I'm fine here, thanks," Joe said.

"You're supposed to be at your desk."

Joe put down his book. "Where is it written down that I have to be at my desk?" he asked. "It's not a rule."

"The school wants the boys to be at their desks

from seven-thirty to nine-twenty," Kevin said. "You know that, Ripley. I don't have to explain it to you."

"It seems pretty arbitrary to me," Joe said. "My mind works whether I'm sitting up or lying down, doesn't it?"

"Let's not get into it now," Kevin said. "Get to your desk. And no Walkman. Okay?"

Joe got off his bed and sat down at his desk.

"Maybe if you'd been at your desk in the first place, you would have understood," Bobby said.

"Leave Ripley alone," Kevin said.

"My pleasure."

As soon as Kevin shut the door behind him, Joe moved back to the bed.

"What makes you think you can get away with breaking the rules?" Bobby asked.

"It's not a rule," Joe said.

"Ludlow's going to make you sweep the halls for a month," Bobby said.

"You going to tell him?" Joe asked. He didn't wait for a reply before putting on his earphones.

Bobby stood and walked to Joe's bed. Without saying a word, he pulled the earphones from Joe's head. "You're supposed to be studying, Ripley. You're supposed to be at your desk, and you're not supposed to be wearing those goddamn earphones."

"Give me back my phones, Katzenbach," Joe said.

"After study," Bobby said. He stuffed the phones in the drawer of his desk and sat down.

Joe leaped from his bed. He gripped the back of Bobby's chair and pushed it to the floor. Bobby went sprawling at the foot of his desk.

"Give me the phones, Wrong Way," Joe yelled. He

reached into Bobby's drawer and pulled out the phones.

"Don't you come near me!" Bobby screamed. "You lousy hamburger face."

"Don't you call me that again," Joe said slowly, making every syllable count. He unclenched his right hand and slapped Bobby just as Bobby was getting to his feet. Bobby staggered backward. His face was beet-red from the imprint of Joe's hand.

The door flew open, and Kevin came in. "What the hell is going on in here?"

"Ripley's been throwing me around," Bobby said. "He pushed me to the floor. He slugged me. You'd better do something about him. He's dangerous."

"What happened, Ripley?" Kevin demanded. "You do it?"

Joe nodded slowly. He looked more dazed than Bobby.

"Why, Ripley?"

Joe said nothing. He continued glaring at Bobby.

"He did it because he's a lousy, stinking hamburger face," Bobby said. "That's why."

"Is that what Katzenbach called you?"

Joe still said nothing.

"The second you left he was lying on his bed, playing his earphones," Bobby said. "All I did was to take them away from him. He pushed me off my chair. When I got up, he slugged me."

"When did you call him Hamburger Face?" Kevin asked.

"It doesn't matter," Bobby cried. "Ripley attacked me."

"Did he call you a name?" Kevin asked. "Did you do anything else to provoke him?"

"I didn't lay a finger on him," Bobby said, ignoring the fact that Joe had called him Wrong Way. He was too ashamed of it to mention it, I knew. "You're going to have to discipline him. You've got to teach him that he can't get violent and get away with it."

"Go back to your desks and start hitting the books," Kevin said. "If you want to talk, we'll talk later."

"Talk?" Bobby asked incredulously. "That's not going to teach him anything."

"Cool it, Katzenbach," Kevin said.

"But he slugged me," Bobby said. "Don't you understand?"

"Why don't you guys consider it a draw?" Kevin suggested.

"I don't believe it," Bobby said.

"Not another word," Kevin said. "From either one of you."

Kevin closed the door behind him.

"Bastard," Bobby said under his breath.

"Going to report me to the Katzenbach Foundation?" Joe asked. "Going to get my scholarship revoked, Wrong Way?"

Bobby said nothing. Nor did Joe. Both of them sat down at their desks. All of us knew that it wasn't over. Not by a long shot.

Chapter 8

All boys should feel free to call on their student counselors. When disagreements arise, boys will find their counselors impartial arbiters in the fair and happy resolution of various problems.

—From the Headmaster's
letter to new boys

When the nine-twenty bell rang, Bobby was usually the first out of the room. But that night Joe left before Bobby had closed his book and put it back on his shelf. So Bobby stayed at his desk, staring at his photographs.

"What are you thinking?" I asked. I closed my poetry reader and pushed my chair away from my desk.

"Can you believe Ludlow?" Bobby asked.

"He was just trying to break up the fight," I said. "If he hadn't come in when he did, Joe might have torn you to pieces."

"He's going to let Ripley get away with it." Bobby sighed. "Ripley beats up on me, and Ludlow lets him off. If it had been me doing the punching, I'd be on social pro for the rest of the term."

"Kevin doesn't have it in for you," I said.

Bobby shrugged. "I bet he calls me Wrong Way behind my back," he said. "How'd Ripley find out about the Wrong Way business? You didn't tell him, did you, Carmichael?"

"Don't worry," I said. "Besides, you got even with the Hamburger Face stuff."

"He deserved it," Bobby said.

"You didn't have to say it."

"Don't get on my case, Carmichael," he said. "You were the one who invented it. Remember? The first day?"

"It was different," I said. "I didn't say it to his face."

"His Hamburger Face, you mean," Bobby said. "I don't know how I keep from puking every time I see that mountain of zits."

"Please, Bobby. Give it a rest."

"I told Billings and Madison your name for Ripley," Bobby said, "last night, when I was upstairs visiting them."

"Why would you do something like that?" I asked.

"I wanted them to know you were okay."

"They probably think I'm a jerk."

"They laughed," Bobby said. "Madison thought it was particularly cool."

"Please, Bobby," I said. "Don't do me any more favors like that. I was sorry about the Hamburger Face stuff as soon as I said it. You should be too."

Bobby wasn't listening to me. "I'm going upstairs to see Billings and Madison. You want to come?"

"Let's go see Kevin," I suggested. "We should talk about it."

"The Face should be around for it," Bobby said. "If Ripley's taking a rain check, so am I."

He looked at the clock on his bureau. It was nine thirty. There was still a half hour till lights out.

"I'll hang around here," I said. "If Joe comes back I can try to work things out."

"You're wasting your time, Carmichael," he said. "Come with me. You'll have a good time."

I sat down on my bunk. "Maybe I'll go to the common room to see what the other guys are up to."

"Suit yourself," Bobby said. "If you want to waste your time with the new boys, that's your problem."

I waited for him to leave. In a moment I heard him running up the stairs to the second floor. I wondered if Bobby thought Billings and Madison really liked him. In the last week or so he had become their after-study gofor; he'd go for their snacks at the canteen, go for their laundry, go for more of the blue notebooks we wrote our homework assignments in.

Kevin's room was next door. From the end of evening study till lights-out his door was open in case anyone wanted to talk with him.

I knocked on the doorframe and waited for him to look up from his book.

"You said we should talk," I said. "Ripley's gone off I don't know where, and Bobby's gone upstairs."

"Why don't you sit down, Cary," Kevin said.

Since the only chair in Kevin's room was the one he was sitting in, I sat at the foot of his bed.

"Who started it?"

"Bobby took Joe's earphones away," I said. "Then Joe pushed Bobby out of his chair. And they called each other names, and then Joe slugged him."

"You were just caught in the middle, huh?"

I nodded, only I didn't feel totally innocent. I wondered what Joe or Kevin would think if they knew I had made up "Hamburger Face." "I guess Bobby and Joe haven't gotten along too well from the word *go*," I said. "I don't know if anything's going to change that."

"Then you'll all have to live with it," Kevin said.

"Couldn't the dean change our rooming assignments?" I asked.

"What sort of reassignment would you suggest?"

"Maybe it would be easier if Joe moved someplace else," I said.

"Not Bobby?"

"Bobby's okay to live with. Joe's the one who got violent."

"All the other rooms are filled," Kevin said. "You know that."

"Joe could swap rooms with someone else," I said. "I bet he would jump at the chance."

"I bet you're right," Kevin said.

"You'll talk to the dean?"

"Rooming assignments aren't my line," Kevin said. "If you want to change roommates, you should talk to your adviser. Then he can go to the dean. If Joe and Bobby want to change, they should see Mr. Martin first too." Mr. Martin, our English teacher, was also our faculty adviser.

"They're the ones who don't get along," I said.

"But they're not doing anything about it," Kevin said. "Maybe you'd better get used to it. You're not the only guys who have ended up at odds. You're not even the first to have an all-out war in the making."

"And I'd better prepare for it to last a whole year?" I asked.

"Unless you want to try moving, you'll have to make a go of it."

"That's it?" I asked. "I feel like I'm stuck in the middle."

"You're friendlier with Bobby, aren't you?"

"Yeah, but Joe and I get along at least."

"It's hard being in the middle," Kevin told me. "But take my advice and stay there. Don't take sides. You'll only make it worse for everyone, including yourself."

"Okay," I said.

So the only solution was to put up with it or pack out. I had expected more from Kevin, and I didn't mind him seeing how disappointed I was.

The clock at the end of the corridor read quarter to ten, and boys were already filing into the bathroom with toilet kits in hand and towels draped over their shoulders. By now I knew everyone's name, where they were from, and how many sisters and brothers each of them had.

"How's it going?" Schumacher asked.

"Okay, Mole. How about you?"

"Some fireworks in your room," he said. "What happened?"

"Bobby and Joe."

"I figured as much. Who won?"

"I don't think there were any winners tonight," I said.

Neither Bobby nor Joe was in the room. If I hurried, I could get into bed before they came back. I could even pretend I was asleep.

After I had closed my eyes and pulled the blanket over my head, someone came into the room. I knew it was Joe because the footsteps stayed on his side of the room. The last bell rang. The man in the powerhouse pulled the switch, and all the lights went out.

I heard footsteps racing down the stairs. They were Bobby's. The metal frame of the bunk beds shook as he hoisted himself to the top.

"Carmichael, you still awake?" he whispered.

"I'm asleep. Don't bother me."

"Guess what happened? Something fantastic."

"Tell me in the morning," I said, rolling over onto my stomach.

"It can't wait till then," he said. "Billings is having trouble with his French homework, so guess what?"

"What?"

"I told him you'd do it for him."

"I have enough trouble doing my own," I said.

"Come on, Carmichael. You're getting A's. You should be honored. You're going to get a lot of points for this one, I can tell you. If I were in French Three, I'd do it myself."

"I don't know how to thank you," I said.

"That's more like it," Bobby said. I heard him rolling over.

From the other side of the room, I heard a low snore. In spite of what had happened, Joe was having no trouble getting to sleep. A little while later Bobby stopped tossing in his bunk. If Bobby was still, it meant he was asleep too.

I stayed awake I don't know how much longer, mad at Bobby and Joe for getting the trouble going, mad at them both for not even trying to make things better. I even put in some time being mad at Kevin, too, for telling me I'd have to wait it out.

Before sleep came, I managed a few moments to resent Bobby for offering my services to Billings. I resented his assuming that I would ever consider doing someone else's homework the opportunity of a lifetime.

Chapter 9

Veritas, honestas, fraternitas.
—Winslow School motto

"I want to talk to you about last night," Joe said as we were walking down the stairs from chapel the next morning.

"Last night?" I asked cautiously. "That's sort of between you and Bobby, isn't it?"

"I didn't mean that stuff," he said. "I meant the French homework. You doing it for Billings?"

"Bobby just got a little overzealous," I said.

"It's cheating," he said. "I know we're not buddies. I just thought someone ought to warn you."

The five-minute bell rang, and Joe and I walked off in opposite directions. Even though I was irritated with Bobby, I was irritated with Joe too. What kind of idiot did he think I was? Didn't he think I was smart enough to know the difference between helping someone and cheating?

That afternoon, after soccer practice, there were tryouts for the Christmas play. It was a musical, an English one called *Riviera Rita*. It took place in the 1920s, and there was a Charleston in it. I knew all the songs because we had the record at home and my mom used to play it a lot. I was hoping I could get one of the smaller parts.

The girls' parts were being played by the Bancroft

girls, and the performances were to be given at Bancroft the two nights before Christmas recess. Although Winslow seemed to have a first-rate everything else, the auditorium at Bancroft was larger and better equipped.

There was a path through the woods that led to Bancroft. I didn't see any other Winslow boys heading in that direction, but when I got to the Bancroft auditorium, there were thirty girls trying out for the eight female parts and eleven boys trying out for the seven male roles. I thought I had a chance, numerically at least.

In the last row sat a girl with bright red hair and a pale complexion. She was wearing jeans, and her feet were planted on the back of the seat in front of her.

"Hi," I mumbled as I sat down two seats away from her.

"Hi, yourself," she said. She put her index finger to her lips and turned her eyes to the stage.

Mr. Martin was standing in the middle of the stage. It turned out he was the faculty adviser to the Winslow Dramatic Society. A few feet away from him, sitting at a small piano, was Miss Ferguson, the faculty adviser to the Bancroft Dramat.

Mr. Martin announced that there were to be three rehearsals a week, one on Wednesday afternoons (which were considered free time because there were no sports then) and on Saturday and Sunday afternoons as well.

One of the boys dropped out. He wasn't going to have time to rehearse. There were now ten boys for the seven parts.

Miss Ferguson played one of the love songs the first leads sing together and then the music to the Charleston. Mr. Martin handed out sheets with the lyrics on them. We were supposed to decide which song we wanted to sing for the audition.

I took the sheet with the Charleston lyrics. So did the red-headed girl.

"My name's Andrea McKaye," she said. "No one ever calls me Andy. Otherwise, I'm not hard to get along with."

"I'm Cary Carmichael. What year are you?"

"Freshman."

"Me too."

The audition began. Billings was there in the first row, and he was the first to go on. He sang the main love song with a beautiful girl with long blond hair that went down to her shoulders. I wondered if she was Wendy Morrison, the girl he and Madison had joked about at dinner.

She was nervous and didn't sing well. Neither did Billings, but it didn't matter. He looked like the son of an English lord (which is what his character was supposed to be), and he was just so darn confident. It was his presence again. It was only an audition, but he looked like he was having a ball while all the other kids were biting their fingernails.

The next couple did the Charleston, but most of the others did the love song. Because there were more girls than boys, Mr. Martin asked Billings and some of the other boys to sing more than once so that all the girls could sing with someone. Even with second chances none of the other boys came close to Billings.

Mr. Martin asked who else was planning on doing the Charleston number. Andrea and I were the only ones to raise our hands. We stood up and walked on-stage. Andrea was two or three inches taller than I was. I had a feeling that we were going to make a pretty funny-looking duo. Miss Ferguson played the introduction.

"When you're feeling blah and bluish . . ." I forgot the words, and Miss Ferguson stopped playing.

"Try a step that's neat and newish," Andrea whispered.

"Try a step that's neat and newish," I sang.

This time I was okay. My voice was a little wobbly, but it was loud, and the lyrics came out okay. Then it was Andrea's turn to get into her part of the introduction.

"To lift the spirits, nothing is diviner than the dance they do in Carolina," she sang. She had a terrific voice, clear and pretty, and her English accent sounded like the real thing.

It was at the beginning of the second chorus that Andrea started doing the Charleston. I started doing an imitation of what she was doing because I really didn't know what the steps were. We heard some giggling, and by the end there was real laughter. When we finished, there was applause and even one bravo. It was from Billings. He was practically falling out of his seat.

Andrea took a bow. So did I. We walked back to our seats.

"Maybe we'll both get parts," I said. I didn't mean those parts specifically, but still, I felt good about it. When the audition ended, Mr. Martin said we would know in a week who got what part. There were going to be some understudies, just in case, and he also said he hoped those of us who didn't get anything would want to help with the sets and props.

"Break a leg, Cary," Andrea said. "Maybe we'll see each other at rehearsals."

I crossed my fingers on both hands and held them up. She smiled and walked off with some of her friends. She was kind of neat, I decided. Most girls would have been self-conscious about being so tall, but she took advantage of it.

I started to walk by myself back to Winslow. The leaves on the path were rustling behind me. Footsteps. They were Billings's, but I didn't know that until he was beside me.

"You guys were great out there," he said. "You two are going to dance off with the show."

"It was Andrea mostly," I said. "She made us both look good."

"It was both of you," he said. "And it was better than good. You should exude a little more confidence, Mr. Carmichael."

If I could have exuded half as much confidence as Billings, I would have been set for life. If I had half his looks, it wouldn't hurt either.

"Look," he said after we had gone a little farther, "there's something I've got to apologize for."

"To me? How come?"

"It's about the French homework," he said. "It was Katzenbach's idea, but you shouldn't blame him. He heard me telling Madison I'd have a much better chance of getting into Peabody if I got my grades up, and he was just being helpful. But I shouldn't have let him ask you, so it's my fault really."

"That's okay," I said, feeling relieved. "I guess I can understand how important getting into a college like Peabody can be."

"And Peabody thinks C's are a disaster area. I'd

drop French altogether if they didn't require a lan
guage credit."

"It's just that I can't do your homework for you,"
said. "It's cheating."

"Katzenbach said I wanted you to do my home
work for me?" he asked.

"You didn't?"

"I'm lousy in French," he said, "but I wouldn't asl
anyone to do my homework for me."

"Not even a lowly freshman?"

"Come on, Cary," he said. "I'm not that desperate
or that stupid. I just need some help, is all."

"I could give you a little help," I said.

"It looks like I'm going to need more than a little
help," he said.

"Like what?"

"Like real tutoring."

"Won't Grady do that for you?"

"It'd be terrible one on one with him," Billing
said. "He'd realize how hopeless I really am."

"Maybe after evening study I could help," I said
"A couple of times a week if you'd like."

"It's a lot to ask."

It was getting darker now. As we turned a corner
in the path, I saw the lights of the school ahead.

"I want to," I said.

"I'll tell you what," he said. "You can work on my
French and I'll work on your self-confidence. Anyone
who speaks French and can do a mean Charlestor
shouldn't have any trouble working up a little more
of the stuff. How's that sound, old buddy?"

It sounded like a terrific bargain to me. So that
night, after evening study, I went up to Billings's
room and worked with him. He really was a disaster

area too. He could barely tell one tense from the other. But after half an hour he began to understand the difference between the *passé composé* and the *imparfait.*

"You're a blooming miracle, Carmichael," he said. "And you're the guy who called himself a lowly frosh just this afternoon, aren't you?"

"You're already doing a lot for my self-image," I said.

"Just keeping up my end of the bargain," he said.

It was almost time for lights-out. I picked up my textbook and papers and started down the hall.

"Cary?"

It was Billings. He was standing in his doorway.

"Thanks," he said. "I mean that."

"Thank you, Billings," I said.

And I meant it too.

10

Chapter 10

The Honor Code
Despite occasional protests to the contrary, the school does not recognize a thin line, much less a gray area, between honesty and dishonesty. Integrity is a matter of black and white, and the school presumes its boys understand the distinction. Our faith in their good judgment is explicit. Boys who do not justify that faith should know they run the risk of expulsion.

—*The Winslow Handbook,*
page 31

Two, maybe three times a week I would go up to Billings's room, and we'd work on his French. Usually Bobby went up with me, and Madison would drop by from his room next door.

"Why are you knocking yourself out with the French?" Madison asked one evening.

"I'm a born overachiever," Billings said. "I want to get into Peabody. Early admission if I can."

"One lousy French grade isn't going to count," Madison said.

"One lousy French grade could make the difference."

"Well, I'm not racking my brain to get into Peabody," Madison said.

"You don't have to," Billings reminded him. "Your

family's been going there for the last ten generations. You were in the day you were born."

"Nice to know social rank still means something, isn't it?" Madison asked. "Right, Katzenbach?"

Bobby chuckled, and he and Madison went back to talking to each other while Billings and I went back to the French. Later, when we were back in our room, Bobby quoted the things Madison had said. Most of them didn't mean anything to me, and I couldn't figure out why he bothered with Madison. Bobby said he just felt comfortable with him.

"Because your families are rich?" I asked.

"Could be part of it," he said. "At least I don't have to apologize whenever I say something."

It was the beginning of the next week when Billings told me to be sure to check out the bulletin board the next day after chapel.

"What's up?" I asked.

"My lips are sealed," he whispered.

"Is it something for all of us?" Bobby asked.

"It affects Cary mostly," he said. "But it should be of interest to all lovers of the theater."

"Is it the cast list?" I asked excitedly.

"Carmichael got the part?" Bobby asked. For the first time he was showing something resembling interest in what I was doing. "Did you get the lead Billings?"

"Okay, you've dragged it out of me, boys," Billings said. "Carmichael and I both are in. But not a word till after chapel. No one's supposed to know. No even me."

The next morning Mrs. Roberts, the Head's secretary, was posting a notice on the bulletin board in

Main. At the top of the list was Billings's name. A little farther down was Andrea's. Then mine.

For about an hour I was a minor celebrity. It seemed like everyone was congratulating me. "Way to go, Carmichael." Every time I heard it, the more I liked it. Not that the Winslow Dramat was any sort of status symbol (Bobby had explained that to me more than once), but freshmen very rarely got to play principal roles. I was thrilled.

I was also getting to feel more self-confident. Billings noticed it and said it proved he was living up to his side of the bargain. I was friendlier with the other guys I was getting to know, starting conversations, not waiting for people to come to me first as I had most of the time. Except I wasn't friendly with Joe Ripley. As long as he stayed out of my way, it was okay.

We had got ourselves into a routine, Joe, Bobby, and I. Wake up in the morning; clean up the room; study in absolute silence in the evening. Except for English class, Bobby and I never heard the sound of Joe's voice.

As it happened, Mr. Martin was talking about adverbs when round two (or was it three?) of the Bobby and Joe match took place. If we could think up a word ending in *ly* which wasn't an adverb, Mr. Martin said he would guarantee a passing grade that semester.

Schumacher raised his hand. "Folly?" he asked.

Mr. Martin raised his eyebrows. "Folly," he repeated under his breath.

"It's a noun," Schumacher said. "Do I pass?"

"I know it's a noun," Mr. Martin said. He shrugged. "I guess you do."

A small cheer went up.

"I guess I should have gone to a different teachers college," he said. "Or maybe a different prep school."

We laughed. Mr. Martin was a Winslow boy himself.

"How about smelly?" Joe asked. "It's an adjective."

"And heavenly," Wilson said. "That's an adjective too."

Mr. Martin leaned back in his chair and held his hands to his face. Even though he was pretending to be crying, he was laughing too.

"I'm calling that teachers college in the morning," he said. "I'm getting my money back."

"Will you share it with us?" Schumacher asked.

"I certainly will not," he said. "You've done enough damage already."

Although we were still in the middle of the class, we heard boys in the hall running up and down. The buzz turned into a soft roar.

"It's D-Day," Mr. Martin said. "The day of reckoning."

"What's going on?" Wilson asked.

"The seniors are lining up for their rating from Peabody."

"What ratings?" Wilson asked.

"Peabody gives ratings to all the boys who've applied," Mr. Martin said. "Today the seniors are finding out if they're in or not. Those who aren't are going to have to start scrambling."

"You know," Bobby said, "Podunk, here I come."

"It's not anything like that," Mr. Martin said.

"Try telling them that," Bobby said.

"If a boy doesn't get into his first-choice college, he'll go someplace else instead," Mr. Martin said.

"And he'll probably get a fine education wherever he goes."

"But no one's going to care," Schumacher said. "No one's going to make any decent contacts at Podunk, so what's the point?"

"The point is you should try to get the best education you can," Mr. Martin said. "Unfortunately some of the seniors don't want to think about that right now. There're bound to be some very disappointed boys around here this afternoon."

"Don't worry," Joe said. "If there're any brokenhearted seniors, Katzenbach can handle them. With Carmichael's help, of course."

"There might be a broken head around here if you keep that up," Bobby said.

"Shove it, Katzenbach," Joe said. "Everyone knows you and Carmichael are the class brownnosers. You guys are always sucking up to Billings and Madison."

"Ripley's using foul language," Bobby said with a smirk. "I think you should have a word with him after class, sir."

"That's enough, Mr. Katzenbach," said Mr. Martin. "You, too, Ripley. I want you all to read the next three chapters of *David Copperfield* by the next class."

There was nothing left to say. Besides, there was no time. The bell rang, and there was the usual racket of chairs being pushed away from desks, notebooks and textbooks being slammed shut, and boys moving toward the door.

Very slowly I put my books in my book bag. Soon Bobby and I were the only boys left in the room. I wondered why Joe had brought me into this mess. Bobby was the one he was supposed to hate.

"We're going to get Ripley for that," Bobby said.

"He's not going to get away with calling us ass kissers."

"What are we supposed to do?" I asked. "Hammer nails through his arms and legs?"

"I'll think of a better plan," Bobby said.

"Let's forget about your plan," I said. "What's the point?"

"But we don't suck up, that's the point."

"We spend some time with Billings and Madison," I said. "Maybe too much time."

"Jeez, Carmichael, don't you understand anything? It's not like we have a choice. We've got to stop Ripley."

"Stop him yourself," I said. "I'm out of here."

"It's not just me against him anymore," Bobby said. "It's you and me."

"You're not making sense," I said.

"We'll meet in the room after lunch," he said. "I'll have some sort of plan then."

"It's your battle," I said. "I couldn't care less what Joe said. He doesn't have anything against me."

"He would if I told him who named him Hamburger Face," Bobby said.

"You're not going to blackmail me, are you?"

"I'll see you after lunch, Carmichael."

Bobby slung his book bag over his shoulder. Without looking back at me, he walked out of the classroom.

Chapter 11

Winslow's academic standards are among the highest in the nation. Of last year's graduating class, almost half went on to Ivy League colleges. Most of the others went on to smaller but otherwise outstanding colleges. One boy enlisted in our armed forces.

—From the Winslow catalog,
page 25

If Bobby worried that our run-in with Joe Ripley would be the big news on campus, he was wrong. That day the only news anyone was interested in was who was in at Peabody and who wasn't. The scene in the dining hall at lunch was mayhem.

Murray jumped in the air when he came in, and half a dozen boys applauded. Early admission. Slocum and Danziger had their arms around each other's shoulders. Marcus took a bow, and all the boys at his table laughed and clapped. Branson just smiled from ear to ear. Everyone expected him to get into Peabody, and he had. More applause. More laughter. Some cheers too.

"Congratulations," Mr. Grady said to Billings as he sat down with the rest of us who were already at the table. Billings was beaming. He didn't have to say it. He was in too.

The bell rang. It was my turn to wait on table. I

joined the line of waiters at the entrance to the kitchen. In another minute I was filing back through the swinging doors with a tureen filled with whatever we would be calling soup that day.

I set the tureen in front of Mr. Grady. As he picked up the ladle, he looked around the table to check that everyone was present.

Everyone was not.

"Is Madison going to be late for lunch?" Mr. Grady asked.

Billings cleared his throat. "Madison isn't going to be joining us, I'm afraid. He's checked into the infirmary."

"Under the weather, is he?"

Billings nodded.

"Bad news from Peabody, I gather," Mr. Grady said as he began to pass the soup bowls. "Poor Madison. His grades just weren't up to snuff. You must be happy, though, Billings."

"I am, sir," Billings said. "Overwhelmed."

"You were surprised?" Grady asked. "Really?"

"Well, my grades aren't the greatest," Billings said. "I wasn't dean's list."

"You've improved very nicely in my class this year," Mr. Grady said. "Don't think I didn't inform the placement office so that they could pass the information on to the admissions office at Peabody."

"Thank you, sir." Billings caught my eye. I felt he was thanking me too.

"Besides, Peabody is always interested in the president of the Student Council. You needn't have worried."

"Who else got in?" Rogers asked.

"Meacham and Durrell," Billings said. "Adkinson

got in. Henry's in too. There are some more who will have to wait till spring to find out. I think that's it for this year."

"Not like the old days," Grady said. "But a perfectly respectable showing nonetheless."

"Did you hear Ludlow got in?" Joe asked.

"Peabody's soccer team must need some beefing up," Denny said.

"Ludlow gets very good grades," Mr. Grady said. "He's got a good head. Good for him."

But for all the boys who were beaming and accepting congratulations, there were as many who were smiling bravely. Even if you weren't a senior, you felt involved. In a year or two or three all of us would be going through the same thing. It was exciting, and it was terrifying.

After my history class I went back to McKinley. The last leaves had fallen from the trees in the quadrangle, and men were busy raking them up. It was beginning to rain. When I got back to the room, Bobby was already there. Ripley's bed was unmade, and the sheets and blanket were lying on the floor.

"I thought you'd forgotten our little appointment," Bobby said.

"I hadn't forgotten, Bobby," I said. "And don't think I'm keeping it either. I'm just dropping my books on my way to soccer practice."

"You don't mind my telling Joe that he has a pretty good reason to hate you?"

"Sure, I mind," I said. "I'm just not giving in to your blackmail, that's all. By the way, what do you think you're doing?"

"I'm pieing Ripley," Bobby said. "You want to lend me a hand?"

"What's pieing?"

"You take one bed," Bobby said. "You remove the top sheet. Then you take the foot of the bottom sheet and draw it up to the pillow. Fold it over the blanket so that it looks like the top sheet. When occupant of aforementioned bed goes to sleep, his feet stop about a foot and half of the way down, giving aforementioned occupant a royal pain. Nice, huh?"

"You'll take full credit for it?" I asked. "I'm bowing out of the Joe Ripley sweepstakes."

"You're going to let that creep call you a brownnoser?" Bobby asked.

"I happen to be rooming with a creep and a blackmailer," I said. "I've decided to take my chances on my own."

"Look," Bobby said, "about the blackmail stuff, it was just me being a little crazy. You know I wouldn't do anything like that, don't you?"

"You had *me* convinced, Bobby."

"You've got to forgive me," he said. "I made a mistake. It'll never happen again. It's just that if we let him get away with it, we're going to be stuck the rest of our lives being called brownnosers."

"It'll pass," I said. "No one's going to remember. No one's even going to care."

"People do care, Carmichael," Bobby said. "It's the sort of thing they care about most. Do you want to end up being the class nerd?"

"Is that something your brother warned you about?"

"He didn't have to," Bobby said. "I'm just not going to let what happened in my old school happen here."

"You were the class nerd in New York?" I asked.

"I've got a chance to make something of myself here," Bobby said.

"What happened?"

"What's it matter?"

"I'm not getting caught up in some problem of yours that happened before I met you," I said. "That's why it matters."

"Oh, hell, Carmichael, it's not that interesting."

"I'm listening, Bobby."

"It was some jerk," he said. "A scholarship kid like Ripley. He told people I wouldn't have been at the school except for my folks and their money. It was sour grapes, but the other kids didn't understand that. They thought it was the only reason I got into Winslow too."

"Pieing Ripley is going to prove you don't need your folks or their money?" I asked.

"I'm just not going to blow it again, and I'm not going to let Ripley blow it for me. It's not my fault he has to work in the faculty Xerox room, is it?"

"What's anything got to do with Joe's bursary job?"

"You've got to watch out for guys like Ripley," Bobby said.

"You, Bobby. Not me. Everything's beginning to go okay for me now," I said. "I'm getting good grades; I've got the part in the play. I don't want to ruin things."

"You know what the worst of it is?" Bobby asked. Clearly he wasn't listening to anything I was saying. "They keep on letting him get away with it. Did you see Martin's face? He wasn't about to say anything to stop Ripley. He's just as bad as Ludlow. They all let Ripley get away with it."

"What do you expect?" I asked. "You think they should put boys on social pro for name-calling. Kevin never reported you for being late the first day, did he?"

"Tell me, Carmichael," Bobby says, "did you do anything to Joe to make him call you a brownnoser?"

I shook my head.

"And if you're honest with yourself, you know that since the slugfest I haven't done anything to him either. Right?"

"True enough."

"So you think he should be able to push us around. Just like that, huh?"

"No," I said. "Of course not."

"Then tuck the other side of the sheet over the blanket, will you?"

I reached out and took hold of the sheet. Bobby never meant it about blackmailing me. He was just this insecure kind of kid who needed a friend and Joe didn't.

That's what I told myself at least.

Chapter 12

November 6

Dear Cary,

If you'd like, why don't you invite Joe Ripley to stay with us during the Thanksgiving holidays? Western Pennsylvania's a long way to go for a four-day recess, and staying at the school can't be very festive.

Congratulations on the play!

Love,
Mom

After I had finished the French homeworks that night, I started in on my algebra. My mind wasn't on it. I tried my Latin. Third-declension nouns. Nothing was sticking. I was thinking about Joe and what he would do when he went to bed that night.

Bobby was scribbling out the first draft of an English essay which was due at the end of the week. As usual, Joe was lying on the bed. His book and his Walkman were in their usual places too. He had studied that way ever since he had slugged Bobby. Although Bobby mentioned it to me three times a week, he never complained to Joe about it again.

The nine-twenty bell rang.

"You going up?" Bobby asked me.

"I guess so," I said. "How about you?"

"I'm going over to the infirmary to check in on

Madison," he said. By then Madison's hospitalization was the hot subject on campus. Everyone was speculating whether getting turned down at Peabody had made him really sick or if he was just faking it.

Joe sat up on his bed and pulled his knees under his chin. "I was right, wasn't I, Katzenbach?" he asked. "You're turning into a regular Florence Nightingale."

"Don't start in on me, Ripley," Bobby said. "You had your say in Martin's class this morning."

"You, Cary?" Joe went on. "Going to hold Billings's hand for a while?"

I shrugged and followed Bobby out into the hall. He slammed the front door of McKinley behind him. I walked up to the second floor.

Three or four seniors were talking in the hall. Billings was sitting in a canvas chair in his room, reading a magazine.

"Bobby's gone over to the infirmary," I said. "He's paying Madison a condolence call."

"Should be a very short visit," Billings said. "Madison isn't receiving visitors."

"Did you see him this afternoon?"

"Only for a minute. I gave him his things, and he told me to get lost."

"Maybe he's feeling better now," I said.

"He'll feel better tomorrow," Billings said. "First thing in the morning his father is getting on the blower—"

"Blower?"

"The telephone," Billings explained. "His father is calling up Peabody. Everything should be straightened out soon. In a day or two Madison will be his old, obnoxious self again."

"What's his father going to say?"

"I guess he's going to read them the riot act," Billings said. "That should get them in line."

"You mean he can make them accept Madison?"

"Mr. Madison can be a very persuasive kind of guy."

"And Peabody will change its mind just like that?"

"Well, it's not as though the Madisons are just off the boat."

"What boat?"

"I mean, it's not as though the Madisons are refugees or anything," Billings said. "They were here practically before the Indians. And they've been going to Peabody forever. Mr. Madison will simply remind them of that little detail, and Peabody will explain they just made a horrible mistake. They'll apologize. Then they'll give Madison early acceptance, and life will go on the way it's supposed to."

"They can do that?"

"They're always doing things like that."

"I didn't know."

"They're very old money," Billings said. "The Madisons can't even remember who was the last person in the family to hold down a job."

"Bobby's father spends his time investing their money," I said. "Doesn't Mr. Madison even do that?"

"Mr. Madison's always doing something," Billings said. "He rides, for instance."

"Horses?"

"Unless some other beast is specified, you can assume riding means horses."

"He does that all day long?"

"He does it every day. But not all day."

"What else?"

"He does volunteer work," he said. "He calls it his special projects, but it's charity."

"For diseases?"

"Mr. Madison doesn't go in for diseases," Billings said. "He thinks they're in bad taste. Mostly he's involved with the SAR."

"What's that?"

"Sons of the American Revolution," he said. "I bet you've never heard of it."

I shook my head.

"I hadn't either. Not until I met Mr. Madison."

"What's he do there?"

"Licks envelopes, I think," Billings said, chuckling. "Mrs. Madison says she really admires people who can rise to the challenge of supporting themselves. Isn't that nice of her?"

Billings and I laughed together.

"You taking Andrea to the mixer?" he asked.

The Bancroft-Winslow mixer was the following Saturday. It was the first mixer of the year. I had thought of asking Andrea, but I wasn't sure I would. I wasn't even sure I would go.

"A little bird told me that Miss Andrea McKaye wouldn't mind at all if you asked her," he said. "You should, you know."

"I might," I said. "You don't need a date to go, do you?"

"You'll have a better time if you do," Billings said. "Why don't you give her a call?"

"Maybe," I said.

"If you don't, I'm going to have to move you back into remedial self-confidence one-oh-one A. I'll write out the phone number of her dorm. You can call her before lights-out."

"Tomorrow maybe," I said.

"Got to get cracking," Billings said. "Otherwise I'll be burning the midnight oil."

He looked at the clock on his desk. It was a quarter to ten.

"There's no time," I said. "I'll help you with the French stuff tomorrow night."

"I've got Student Council tomorrow," he said. "I don't know how I'm going to make the time."

"We should have started with the work and then talked," I said.

"Look, Cary, maybe you could let me see your homework. Just this once. What with the play and the council I don't have the time."

"It's cheating," I said. "You said you'd have to be desperate and stupid to do it."

"Okay, I'm not stupid. But I'm desperate. If you don't help me this once, I don't know what else I can do."

"We'll get caught," I said. "Grady will know one of us is copying."

"I'll make some mistakes," Billings said. "He'll never guess."

"Even with my tutoring you're not up to knowing which mistakes to make without making Grady suspicious."

"Then you make the mistakes for me," he said.

"What do you mean?"

"After you've done your usual A-plus homework, you can make another with all the mistakes you think I should make. Just make sure I get a B at least."

"I don't like it," I said. "I just don't know."

I walked down the corridor. When I got to the bottom of the stairs, I saw Kevin in his room.

"I wanted to congratulate you on Peabody," I said.

"Thanks, Cary."

"You must be pretty excited about going," I said.

"Well, it's nice to get in," he said. "But I've applied to a couple of other places, and I still have to hear from them."

"You may not go to Peabody?"

"I haven't made up my mind."

"You've got to be the only one around here who wouldn't jump at the chance to go there," I said.

"It's a big decision. Maybe I just wanted to see if I could get in. I don't know."

"Congratulations anyway."

"How are you doing, Cary? Are you staying in the middle?"

"Of Bobby and Joe, you mean?"

"Yeah."

"I'm trying," I said. "I don't know how well I'm doing."

When I got back to my room, the last bell rang and the lights went out. I groped my way to my bed. It wasn't until the next morning that I realized Joe hadn't made a scene about the pieing. He hadn't even mentioned it. Even so, I wasn't about to ask him to spend the Thanksgiving recess with my folks. The next night, during evening study, I wrote them that Joe had other plans.

Then I made two copies of the next day's French homework, one for me and the other for Billings. I knew that if Billings turned in his own homework, it would be so awful that it would arouse Mr. Grady's curiosity, if not suspicions. I knew it was wrong, but I had to help Billings. Besides, thanks to Billings's plan, there was no way either of us could get caught.

It didn't make it right. I knew that even then. But it made it possible. Two days later, when Mr. Grady returned the homeworks, I got my usual 94 and Billings got his usual 83. I needn't have worried. I should have known that things always worked out fine for Billings.

Chapter 13

Attention: All Boys

The first Winslow-Bancroft mixer of the year will take place this Saturday in the Winslow dining hall. A "rock" band has been engaged for the occasion, but boys will dress appropriately—tie and jacket. We hope a convivial evening will be had by all.

—The Head

Even though Billings said Andrea would accept, I was nervous about calling her. We'd been rehearsing the show for almost a month, which meant I'd seen her a dozen times since the audition, but inviting a girl to the mixer was close enough to a real date to make me anxious: anxious that she'd decide she didn't want to come with me (in spite of what Billings had said) and anxious she might accept and I'd turn out to be the biggest flop of the year.

But I screwed up my courage, called her from the pay phone in Main just before breakfast (when nobody was around), and when she accepted, I wondered what the big deal was. It was just a mixer after all.

Bobby was already at breakfast when I got to the dining hall.

"Get your grub," he said. "I've saved a seat for you."

He was the only one at the table, but I wasn't sure he was kidding, so I didn't laugh. I got my juice, some milk, and a box of cornflakes.

"I couldn't find you," he said. "Where'd you disappear to?"

"I didn't disappear," I said. "I wanted to invite Andrea to the mixer."

"Hey, Schumacher," Bobby said, waving his hand in the air, "we saved you a seat."

Schumacher sat down across from us. Taggart and Dreyfuss joined us too.

"Why do you want to go to the mixer?" Bobby asked.

"Sounded like fun," I said.

"Isn't McKaye too tall for you?"

"It doesn't bother me," I said.

"It would me," Bobby said. "You going, Taggart?"

"I don't know yet," Taggart said.

"How about you, Dreyfuss?"

"Probably. Nothing else to do except go to the movie, and I've already seen it."

"You know what they call the mixers, don't you?" Bobby asked. He looked around the table. When no one answered, he looked triumphant. "They're called the pig pools." Bobby started giggling. No one joined in. "Don't you guys bother to wake up before breakfast? That's what my brother called them. Pig pools!"

"Your brother didn't go to the mixers?" Schumacher asked.

"How would I know?" Bobby said. "What difference does it make?"

"You don't need a date to go, do you?" Schumacher asked.

"You can, but you don't have to," I said.

"I guess I'll go," Schumacher said. "I don't know anyone at Bancroft to ask."

"I got an idea, Carmichael," Bobby said. "We've got a weekend pass to use up before the end of term. What say you and me go to New York? My folks are in Bermuda. We can have their place to ourselves."

"I already asked Andrea to the mixer," I said. "I told you."

"I didn't know she said yes," Bobby said, looking put-out. "How about you, Taggart? You want to go to New York? How about you, Dreyfuss? The three of us could have a neat time."

"I'd sort of like to see what a mixer is like," Dreyfuss said.

"Why don't *you* go to the mixer, Bobby?" I asked. "A lot of girls at Bancroft are nice-looking. You know that."

"Sounds like a drag," Bobby said. He turned toward Taggart. "My father's secretary can get us tickets to a Jets game. Or maybe a show. How about it?"

"Shows are expensive," Dreyfuss said.

"They'll be free," Bobby said. "Dad's secretary can write them off."

"No, thanks," Dreyfuss said. "I'll stick around here."

"Well, you guys do what you want," Bobby said. "I'm going to New York, and I'm going to have one terrific time too. Anyone who changes his mind can come. Okay?"

"You could change your mind too," I said.

"Yeah, but I'm not going to," Bobby said.

"Why not?"

"Lay off, will you, Carmichael?" He scrunched his paper napkin and dropped it in the middle of his plate. He got up and walked out of the dining hall.

"Wonder why Katzenbach's so uptight about the mixer," Schumacher said. "He have something against girls?"

"How would I know?"

"You're his roommate, Carmichael," Taggart said.

"'Let me tell you all about our apartment on Park Avenue,'" Schumacher said, aping Bobby. "'Let me tell you about our weekend place on Long Island and our château in France.' Why doesn't Wrong Way give it a rest?"

"The guy gives snobs a bad name," Taggart said.

"He's okay," I said. "His brother said the mixers were pig pools, is all."

"Spare me," Taggart said. "I've heard enough about Peter Katzenbach Boy Wonder to last me a lifetime."

"You think Wrong Way's scared of girls?" Schumacher asked. "Maybe he's a social retard or worse."

"Gee," Dreyfuss said, "maybe there's something seriously wrong with Wrong Way."

The boys laughed, and I stood up. They didn't know Bobby as well as I did, but there wasn't anything I could say for him. I knew Bobby tried too hard to impress people, but that was the first time I found out you didn't have to be Joe Ripley to dislike Bobby Katzenbach.

Saturday afternoon the cast rehearsed over at Bancroft. We had our first run-through, and afterward we tried on our costumes. I was wearing a red-and-

white-striped blazer, white ducks, white shoes, and a
boater with a red-and-white-striped ribbon around
the brim. Andrea was wearing a flapper dress, a head-
band, and strings of fake pearls that came down to
her knees. We admired ourselves in the mirror in the
back of the auditorium. Even if she was three inches
taller than I was, I thought we made a pretty smart-
looking couple.

"I'm not going in flats tonight," she said as she in-
spected herself. "I'm going to wear heels. Is that okay
with you, Cary?"

"They'll make you look taller," I said.

"That's why I'm asking," she said. "It's also going
to make you look a little shorter. I say if you've got it,
flaunt it. If you mind, though, I'll wear flats."

"Wear the heels," I said.

"You must be pretty sure of your masculinity," she
said.

"What are you talking about?"

"It's in Joyce Brothers," she said. "Men who are
comfortable about themselves don't worry about
things like women being taller."

"I didn't know that," I said.

"Now you do," she said, winking at me.

Then it hit me, a really sensational idea. "Let's
wear the costumes to the mixer."

"You're getting worse than I am," Andrea said.
"You're kidding, aren't you?"

"Why not? It's okay with the dress code. Ties, jack-
ets, dresses. We'll just be a little flashier than the others."

"If you're game, I am too," she said. "But I'll wear
flats."

"You don't have to if you don't want to," I said,

feeling almost as secure in my masculinity as Joyce Brothers and Andrea thought I was.

"I want to wear flats," she said.

So we arranged to meet after dinner when the Bancroft bus would pull up to Main. The dining room had been cleared and a small rock band was playing at one end and there was a refreshment stand at the other end. Luckily for us it was a cold night, and we all were wearing overcoats. I kept my boater hidden under my coat. Andrea and I wanted to save our surprise.

The boys who had already arranged for their dates met the girls in front of Main and walked them to the dining hall. The others who were on their way drifted in separate groups across the quadrangle.

I was about to hang up my coat in the anteroom when Andrea stopped me.

"You're not going to take off your coat yet, are you?" she asked.

"Why not?"

"We've got to make an entrance," she said. "We have to wait until everyone else gets to the dining hall."

Andrea knew a thing or two that I didn't. But the fact was that I was having fun before the dance began.

"What if they send us back for some real clothes?" I asked.

"They wouldn't dare," Andrea said. "We're going to be a smash."

Andrea's enthusiasm was contagious. After all, it had got us the parts in *Riviera Rita*. I could hardly wait till we made our entrance.

From the anteroom we could see the boys and girls

with dates begin to dance. Some of the others were standing at the refreshment table and starting to mingle. Somehow I was surprised that a Winslow dance was a lot like a dance back home. I would have thought that the boys and girls here would have looked a lot more sophisticated. I remembered that if it weren't for Andrea, I might not have been at the dance at all.

"Now?" I asked.

Andrea nodded and we hung up our overcoats. When we walked into the dining hall, I wasn't sure at first if anyone noticed us. When we started to dance, however, a crowd gathered around us and some of the kids began to clap and say 1920s things like "twenty-three skiddoo" and "cat's pajamas." When the music stopped, there was more applause. Show-offs that we were, we took a bow and made our way to the refreshment table.

"Well, will you get a load of that?"

It was Billings, and he was walking toward us through the crowd. There was an enormous smile on his face. He stood between Andrea and me. For a second I thought he was going to ask Andrea to dance, but he didn't. I didn't know how Andrea felt about it, but I was relieved. I didn't think I could stand the competition.

"Got something special in store for us tonight?" Billings asked us.

"This is it," I said.

"What are we supposed to do, Alec?" Andrea asked. It was funny, but I had never heard anyone call Billings by his first name before.

"Leave it to me, kids," he said, and walked off.

"You have any idea what he's up to?" Andrea asked.

"None at all," I said.

The music started again, and Andrea and I danced some more. She introduced me to her roommate, Cynthia Porter, who was dancing with Mole Schumacher. I danced with Cynthia while Mole and Andrea danced. The music was too loud for us to talk.

The band broke for intermission, and most of the boys and girls headed back to the refreshment table. I joined Andrea again, and we had some punch.

"Attention, attention!" Billings called from the center of the hall. "We've got a special treat this evening, guys and gals," he said. "Something you won't want to miss. We're going to have a sneak preview of the showstopping number from *Riviera Rita.* It's the big Charleston number."

I felt a nervous knot forming in my throat. I looked at Andrea, who was as dumbfounded as I was. The Charleston number. That meant us!

"So may I introduce those crazy madcaps from the Roaring Twenties, Andrea McKaye and Cary Carmichael. Miss Ferguson, please!"

With almost two hundred people looking on, there was no way Andrea and I could bow out. Besides, it had happened too quickly for us to build up a full-scale case of nerves. Miss Ferguson started the introduction, and the kids formed a circle around Andrea and me.

Only vaguely aware that I was singing the right words or the right notes, I started. Andrea lost her nervousness by the time we got to the chorus, and by the time we got to the Charleston itself, we both were having a ball. By popular demand we gave an encore. Afterward there were cheers all around.

Andrea and I were exhausted but thrilled. I wondered if maybe I hadn't been hoping something like this might happen. It was wonderful: all the attention; the applause; the feeling that we were really a part of what was going on. We belonged there.

At ten o'clock the girls got their coats, and the boys walked them across the quadrangle to the Bancroft bus. I kissed Andrea. It was awkward. I almost got her ear, but she didn't mind. We would see each other at the next rehearsal.

Because of the mixer, the boys were allowed to stay up until ten-thirty that night, but it was almost that when I got back to the room. I was more than happy. I was elated. I didn't miss Bobby. I hardly remembered that he had gone home for the weekend.

"Have a good time at the mixer?" I asked Joe.

"Pretty good," he said. "Not so good a time as you."

"Yeah," I said. "I had a lot of fun. Are you going to see the show?"

"Maybe," he said. "You were good, Cary. Really good."

It was more praise than I had ever expected from him. But probably Joe wouldn't have said anything if Bobby had been there. I know I wouldn't have said anything to Joe.

Chapter 14

Carmichael, Cary   Year: Fresh.
McKinley No. 4   Adviser: Mr. Martin

Algebra I   82
English I   85
French III 94
History I   86
Latin I   78

Very commendable midterm report, Cary. Good showing on the French. Mr. Grady reports you are an industrious student.

—Allan Martin

Midterm grades came out the next week, and Bobby and I went to pick up our report cards at Mr. Martin's office on the second floor of Main. Before we got back down to the second floor, I had taken the report from the envelope and was figuring out its net worth when it came to being a preppie scholar. I was disappointed by the algebra and relieved about the Latin. Everything looked good or better than good.

To make dean's list, I needed an 85 average. Before we had headed for Mr. Martin's office, I had figured out that my grades would have to add up to a total of 425. I had made it, but with nothing to spare. I trembled a little at my luck.

"How'd you do?" I asked Bobby as we got to the landing.

"Who cares?"

"You're not interested?"

Bobby took his report card from the envelope. Without even looking at it, he handed it to me. His grades were mostly in the low seventies, except for algebra, which he was flunking. Mr. Martin's note said that Mr. Wilkins, the algebra teacher, was setting up tutorial sessions for him.

"Not all that bad," I said. "Except for the algebra, and you'll do okay with some tutoring."

"Do me a favor, Carmichael," he said. "Don't try to cheer me up."

"You shouldn't have a heart attack about it," I said.

"How'd you do?" he asked. "Dean's list?"

"Just barely."

"Just barely counts," he said. "My brother Peter was dean's list all the way through Winslow."

"Good for him," I said, knowing that I should have assumed his brother was a superstar student as well as a superstar athlete. "Look, Bobby, no one's expecting you to be just like your brother."

"My folks wouldn't mind if I were," he said.

"Come on. Take it easy on yourself."

"I'll probably get an earful this weekend," he said. "I'd even be willing to take bets on it."

"You're going to New York again this weekend?"

"They're coming here," Bobby said. "There's a trustees' meeting on Saturday night after the Taft game. They're taking me out for lunch on Sunday. You want to come along?"

"Is that an invitation?"

"The food's supposed to be pretty good at the
Winslow Inn, you know."

"Did your folks say it was okay to invite someone?" I
asked.

"It'll be okay," Bobby said. "They're not going to
do a number on me if you're around."

"You want me there to run interference?"

"Please, Carmichael. I'd do the same for you."

As we walked into the lobby of Main, Miss Saun-
ders from the headmaster's office was tacking something on the bulletin board. It was the dean's list. I
looked for my name under the freshman class list. It
was there.

"Jeez," Bobby said. "Who'da thunk it?"

"Huh?"

Bobby pointed to the top of the list: "High Honor
Roll." Under it was Joe Ripley's name. He was the
only freshman on it.

It didn't help matters, of course, but at least it kept
Bobby from complaining to me anymore about Joe's
lying on his bed and listening to his Walkman during
evening study.

"I wonder how he gets away without studying,"
Bobby said to me the day before the Katzenbachs
were to take us out to lunch.

"He's studying, Bobby," I said. "He's got to be.
Even with the Walkman."

"Yeah, sure," Bobby said sarcastically.

"Face it," I said. "Joe happens to be very, very
bright."

"I don't care," he said. "It's not fair, that's all."

"I bet that's the first time you ever thought life was
unfair," I said.

"You know what I mean," he said.

Bobby ignored me and walked into town to visit his parents, who were staying at the Winslow Inn with the rest of the trustees. When they brought him back to school, they stopped by the room on their way to the private dinner the headmaster was having.

What surprised me most was how young they were. They looked like they had just stepped out of an ad for the Bahamas, which wasn't all that surprising, since they were spending a lot of their time there that fall.

The next day the Katzenbachs attended Sunday chapel at the school, and afterward they drove Bobby and me to the inn in their Mercedes. I guessed that their limousine was in the shop for repairs, or maybe it was the chauffeur's day off.

"Roast beef for the boys," Mr. Katzenbach said to the waiter after we had sat down. "Shrimp cocktail first maybe. How does that sound, boys?"

"Why not let the boys order for themselves?" Mrs. Katzenbach asked. "They know how to read the menu, Teddy."

"Peter always swore by the roast beef here," he said. "I assumed Bobby and his friend would want the same."

"Have whatever you'd like, boys," Mrs. Katzenbach said.

Bobby looked at the menu. "I'll have the roast beef I guess. And the shrimp cocktail too."

"I'd like the same, please," I said.

Mrs. Katzenbach ordered a Bloody Mary and Caesar salad. Mr. Katzenbach ordered a manhattan (straight up) and the cannelloni. I looked around the

dining room. It was very pretty, nice and old-fash-
ioned, with a huge fireplace at the other end.

"Bobby says your father is a college professor,"
Mrs. Katzenbach said.

"He teaches French," I said. "At Stanton College.
It's about a hundred miles west of here."

"I know of it," she said. "It has a very nice reputation."

For want of anything to say, I nodded.

"It's in Pennsylvania, did you say?" Mr. Katzenbach asked.

"New York, dear," Mrs. Katzenbach said.

"Western Massachusetts," I said.

There was an awkward pause.

"Maybe we're thinking of another Stanton Col-
ege," Mr. Katzenbach said at last.

"Maybe you're thinking of two other Stanton Colleges," Bobby said. He held a fork up to his mouth
and bit into a jumbo shrimp. He ignored the look his
mother was giving him. His father took a sip of his
manhattan. Apparently he didn't care one way or another.

"Peter's going to be joining us for Thanksgiving,"
Mrs. Katzenbach said.

"Where else would he be going?" Bobby asked.

"Didn't he tell you?" Mrs. Katzenbach asked. "He
and his roommate were thinking of going to Aspen
for the skiing. Peter is Bobby's older brother," she
said to me.

I nodded.

"He's at Princeton," she said. "I suppose you know
that too."

"Cary even knows where Princeton is," Bobby
said.

He giggled. I tried very hard not to crack a smile

"Are you making a joke at your mother's expense?"
Mr. Katzenbach asked Bobby.

"Just a joke," he said. "No one's expense. It's jus
that Cary's very smart. He made dean's list."

For someone who was worried about his grades
Bobby was courting disaster, I thought. I knew it wa
no accident, though. He had decided to force it on hi
folks.

"Congratulations, Cary," Mrs. Katzenbach said
"You must work very hard."

"Which is more than anyone can say about me,
guess," Bobby said.

"That's not true," I said. "You study all the time
Bobby."

Bobby did study as much as anyone else and harde
than most, but it was the wrong thing for me to say
All that studying and not very much to show for it

"Have you arranged for the tutoring yet?" his fa
ther asked.

"Twice a week," Bobby said.

"Very good," Mr. Katzenbach said. "You'll have
licked in no time. How's the roast beef, boys?"

"Very nice," I said. "It's delicious."

"Aren't you disappointed?" Bobby asked. "In m
grades, I mean."

"You'll do better," his father said.

"Not as well as Peter did when he was at Win
low," Bobby said.

"Peter's a natural student," Mrs. Katzenbach said
"You have other areas of strength."

"Name one," Bobby said.

"Please, Bobby," his mother said. "Don't mak
things worse than they have to be."

"Does that mean you pass on the question?" Bobby asked. "Where do you think my areas of strength lie, Dad?"

"Well," Mr. Katzenbach said, "I wouldn't say your table manners fit into that category."

From the look on Bobby's face I could tell that Mr. Katzenbach had won that round hands down. As for myself, I just wanted to leave. Sitting in on another family's quarrels wasn't doing anything for my appetite.

Mrs. Katzenbach changed the subject to the health of Bobby's grandfather. From there we went on to the wedding plans of one of his cousins. By the time we got to dessert I knew about the rotten Arab sheikh in their apartment building who was turning Park Avenue into a slum, the handball finals at the New York Athletic Club, and the weather in Acapulco this time of year.

"They're a dose, aren't they?" Bobby asked after his parents had dropped us off back at school.

"You kind of baited them," I said.

"Come on, Carmichael. You're not talking sense."

"You were practically asking them to put you down."

"Don't you get it?" Bobby asked. "I don't have to ask for it. It's there all the time. I'm just bringing it out in the open, getting them to say what they really mean."

"You're not being fair to them," I said. "Or to yourself."

"It hasn't anything to do with being fair," he said. "The world's full of jerks like me who have all the advantages and never measure up. I study as hard as anyone else, you said so yourself, and what do I get for it? I invite the guys home, and no one wants to come. Sometimes I think there's some kind of jinx on me."

"You're just having a little trouble right now. It's going to work out okay. Give yourself a chance."

"I see these guys at this country club we belong to," he said. "They have everything going for them, but they can't cut the mustard. Just like me. Only they're forty years old and they're sloshed all the time. If they're lucky, they drop dead of a heart attack on the tennis court. I know this one guy. He defenestrated."

"Huh?"

"You know, out the window. Splat. All over the pavement."

"That's not you. Not really."

"Sometimes I think it could be me," he said.

I let him walk ahead of me into McKinley. He wanted to be alone now, and so did I. I guess I just needed a little time to let it sink in that I really felt for the guy. I wondered if anyone but me ever felt sorry for a millionaire.

Chapter 15

November 29

Dear Mrs. Katzenbach,
  Thank you very much for lunch last Sunday at the Winslow Inn. The food was delicious, and I enjoyed meeting you and Bobby's dad.
  My family had a real nice Thanksgiving.

Sincerely,
Cary Carmichael

The holiday had gone off okay, talking to my old friends on the phone, going out with them on Friday night and Saturday, eating everything in the fridge I could lay my hands on, but I was glad to be back at Winslow. It was like coming home, except for the fact I'd just come from home. It was a kind of shock, realizing my life was centered at Winslow now.

When I got to McKinley, there were lights coming from Kevin's room and mine. Bobby, I knew, was planning another one of his late entrances. It must be Joe. I expected to find him lying on his bed, his earphones on and a paperback propped on his stomach. But when I walked into the room, he was unpacking a suitcase.

"Hi," I said as I dropped my own suitcase on my bunk. "Have a nice holiday?"

"Okay," he said. "Real nice."

"Do you have relatives around here?" I asked.

"I've got an aunt in Manchester," he said.

"That's nice."

"You really interested?"

"Sorry," I said.

He closed the bureau drawers and lifted his suitcase to the top shelf of the closet.

"Is something wrong?" I asked.

"I'm a little uptight, that's all."

"Something to do with me?" I asked. "The weekend of the mixer I thought we were beginning to get along."

"Sure, and we both know why."

I shook my head.

"Because Katzenbach wasn't around," Joe said. "Whenever he's gone, it's okay between us. When he's here, it's hell."

"And you figure it's all Bobby's fault?"

"See? You're taking his side again."

"Just because Bobby and I are friendly doesn't mean I don't see his shortcomings," I said. "His being rich isn't his fault, and it isn't his fault that you've got a chip on your shoulder. If you got to know him a little better, you'd know his life isn't so terrific."

"He gives me a pain," Joe said.

"And that gives you the right to call us both brownnosers," I said. I hadn't intended to say anything about that again ever. I never wanted to remember that scene in Mr. Martin's class.

"Look, I'm sorry about that," Joe said. "I've been meaning to apologize for that. To you. Not Katzenbach."

"Why did Bobby deserve it?"

"I owed him one for the Hamburger Face," Joe said.

"And he owed you one for the Wrong Way," I said. "And for slugging him."

"I owed him that for ripping my headphones," Joe said. "And I still owe him one for pieing my bed one night. You know about that, Carmichael? Katzenbach pied my bed. I couldn't believe it. I don't think they even do that at summer camps anymore."

I shrugged. As far as I could tell, there wasn't any reason to let Joe know I had been involved with the pieing and the Hamburger Face stuff.

"So it's just Bobby," I said. "If it weren't for him, you think we would have gotten along better?"

"Maybe. Maybe not," Joe said. "Sometimes you're kind of a patsy. I don't like that much."

"I'm not," I said.

"About the Billings stuff you are," he said.

"What are you talking about?"

"The way you and Katzenbach run up the stairs when the nine-twenty bell rings," he said. "At least you had the sense not to get mixed up in doing Billings's homework for him. See what kind of friend Katzenbach is? What kind of friend is that?"

If there had been a carpet in McKinley No. 4, I would have considered crawling under it. There I was letting Bobby take the blame for the pieing and the Hamburger Face. That was bad enough. But I couldn't let Joe know that I had let Billings copy a homework even once. He wouldn't have understood.

"One of the reasons I was friendly with Bobby was that he needed a friend," I said. "You act like you never need anyone."

"Maybe the chip on my shoulder, the one you were talking about, was showing," Joe said.

"A chip against me?"

"Your dad's a professor," he said. "That impressed the hell out of me."

"I never thought anyone would be impressed," I said. "Not around here, where half the parents are millionaires."

"So now you know a little more about me," he said. "Maybe we could be friends."

"That would be nice."

"I'm glad we talked, Cary," he said. "I think we're on firmer ground now."

"Yeah," I said, but I had a definite feeling that I was stumbling into quicksand.

Chapter 16

December 1

Dear Cary,
Sandra Burlingame asked her mother to ask me to ask you if you'd take her (Sandra, not her mother) to a dance at their country club during Christmas. I gave her a tentative yes until I get the official go-ahead from you. She (Sandra's mother, not Sandra) says Winslow boys are the best catch.

Love (and congratulations!)
from your social secretary,
Mom

The day after we got back from Thanksgiving we were supposed to sign up for winter sports. What we had to choose from were hockey, basketball, wrestling, swimming, riflery, and squash.

"Bring your skates with you?" Bobby asked me after lunch.

"I don't own a pair," I said.

"Well, you'll have to go into Springfield and buy some, then," he said.

"I'm not going out for hockey," I said. "I don't skate very well. Besides, it's cold out there in the afternoons. I was thinking of doing something indoors this winter."

"Indoor sports are for nerds," Bobby said.

We were standing on the steps to the gym. As we reached the top, the doors swung open and three seniors with skates over their shoulders came out.

"Muldaur, Evans, and Kirk," Bobby said.

"I know who they are, Bobby."

"They're going out for hockey," he said. "And they're all A-list boys."

"I just don't want to play hockey," I said.

"You're not thinking of riflery, are you?" Bobby asked. "It's not even a sport, really."

We walked down the main corridor of the gym. It felt like it was about 112 degrees. I loosened my scarf and unbuttoned my parka.

"I was thinking of basketball," I said.

"Almost as bad as riflery," Bobby said.

"It's what I did back home," I said.

"Me too," Bobby said. "But they didn't have ice hockey at my school in New York."

"Did your brother play hockey at Winslow?"

"First team."

"Why don't you do something different from your brother?" I asked. "Sooner or later you should stop competing with him."

"I want hockey," Bobby said, looking determined again.

"I'll stick with basketball. Hockey's in your genes. Not mine."

"It's your funeral," Bobby said.

"I like playing basketball," I said. "I'm not bad at it either."

"Don't worry, Carmichael. I'll tell you about all the hockey games. You can get your thrills vicariously."

"You'll tell me about all the A-list friends you make, too, won't you?"

"It will be my pleasure," he said. "And you can tell me about all the nerds you meet at basketball practice. Ripley especially."

"Joe's going out for basketball?"

"I said it was the sport of nerds, didn't I?" Bobby said. "I saw him buying his own little basketball this morning at the school store. Maybe his family has a little basketball hoop nailed up over their garage. Just like the Brady Bunch."

"You don't have to be so rough on Joe," I said. "Yesterday, before you got back, we had a nice talk."

"I don't believe it," Bobby said. "You've been consorting with the enemy."

"We're not enemies," I said. "You just decided that the first day of school."

"Look, Carmichael, just the sight of that guy's Hamburger Face makes me want to throw up."

"It isn't that bad."

"It is, and you know it. You said so yourself."

"Well, he's not that bad," I said. "He said some things that got me thinking."

"About me?"

"About me."

"He likes you?"

"He doesn't hate me."

"You'd like to be friends with him?"

"I'd like us all to get along better," I said.

"Then, you're on your own, kid," he said. "I wouldn't want to be caught dead with that nerd. When you come to your senses, you'll know where to reach me."

We were standing at the end of the corridor. To our right the lines were forming for each sport.

"Basketball's over there," Bobby said, pointing to the line forming at the far end.

"I see it, Bobby."

I started to walk over to it.

"You're making a big mistake, Carmichael," Bobby called.

"About basketball?"

"That too," he said as he walked toward the hockey line.

Maybe he was right. But from now on I was going to make my own mistakes and not let Bobby Katzenbach make them for me.

The Winslow Blues threw basketballs around for an hour. I took a shower. There was just enough time to get to Bancroft for the rehearsal. Most of the time, though, Andrea and I talked about our vacations. Billings didn't show. I asked about him, but no one knew where he was.

He showed up for dinner, though, and he was with Madison. For two guys who were on their way to Peabody they didn't look very happy. Madison was more peevish than ever, and Billings looked edgy.

"You boys are preparing for your exams, I trust," Mr. Grady said as we dug into our chipped beef on toast. It was only when Grady wasn't around that we called it shit on a shingle.

Most of the boys nodded. Madison didn't.

"What's the point?" he asked.

"The point is that good grades are better than bad ones," Mr. Grady replied.

"Doesn't make much difference to me anymore," Madison said.

Mr. Grady must have had an answer for that. He must have had dozens, but he only frowned.

"I mean it's a joke," he said persistently.

"Cool it, Madison," Billings said.

"Cool it yourself," Madison said with a sneer. "And just shut up. You're in Peabody, so good grades or bad grades or just plain indifferent grades don't mean a thing to you. You just have to graduate from this dump and you're home free."

Mr. Grady and the others stared at their chipped beef.

"But you're in at Peabody," I said.

Madison shook his head.

"Didn't your father talk to them yet?"

"It was no dice," Madison said. "They turned me down flat. I think my father should get his money back. Don't you agree, Mr. Grady, sir?"

"I don't think I follow you," Mr. Grady said.

"Since I didn't get into Peabody, this place hasn't been worth the four years I've spent here," Madison said. "Or the forty grand it cost my father."

"Winslow School doesn't offer money-back guarantees," Mr. Grady said. "We're an institution of learning. We're not Procter and Gamble."

"This place sucks," Madison said.

"That will be all, Madison," Mr. Grady said. "In spite of your best efforts, you probably have learned a thing or two here. But the credit for that goes to the school, not to you, Madison. You are excused."

"Anybody want to join me for a smoke in the quadrangle?" Madison asked.

"Please, Madison," Mr. Grady said, "don't. All the boys know smoking is against all the rules."

"I beg your pardon, boys," Madison said sarcastically. "I beg yours, too, Mr. Grady, sir. I'll take my evening stroll by myself."

As he turned from the table, he pulled a lighter from the breast pocket of his blazer. Then he pulled out a joint. He stuck it in his mouth and lighted it.

"You're a fool, Madison," Mr. Grady said, his voice rising.

"Sorry," he said. "I'd love to stay and chat, but I really must fly now."

Grady rose from his seat, but otherwise he was as immobilized as the rest of us. By the time Madison got to the main door of the dining hall, the Headmaster and two of the other masters were surrounding him. They were the ones who led him out the door.

It was just before evening study that Billings rapped on our door. Bobby was still not back, but Joe was there, writing his weekly letter to Sherry back home in Pennsylvania.

"Sorry to bother you," Billings said to me. "Madison's in a bad way. They're expelling him. I have to talk with him. Could you get a copy of the French homework to me before lights out?"

Joe turned around at his desk and looked at me.

"It's an easy assignment," I said to Billings. "You're not going to have any trouble with it."

"But I won't have time," Billings said. "You guys saw what happened at dinner tonight."

I nodded, but I didn't mean I was going to do the homework for him. I couldn't with Joe there.

"Thanks, old buddy," Billings said. "It means a lot to me."

He left the room before I could say anything more. I looked helplessly at Joe.

"You've been doing the homework all along for him, haven't you?"

"Once," I said. "That's all."

"So you're really an ass kisser after all," he said.

"I'm not kissing anyone's ass," I said. "I was helping him out. I knew you wouldn't understand."

"The problem is, I do understand," Joe said. "You cheated for him just so that he would like you."

"I have to do it tonight," I said. "You saw Madison."

"I think you're addicted to Billings," Joe said. "You need him to feel good about yourself. Taking him the homework is how you get your fix."

"You take it up, Joe," I said. "That should show you I don't do it for some kind of pat on the back from Billings." With Joe there accusing me like that, there was nothing else I could say. "Come on, Joe. Take it up."

After a pause, he said, "Okay, Cary. I'll take the homework up for you this one time. But I want you to stop this nonsense, okay? You're too smart a guy to be such a jerk."

"Okay," I said.

Even though he didn't understand, I knew he wanted what was right for me. Sometimes everyone does something right for the wrong reasons.

Or was that supposed to go the other way around?

Chapter 17

December 12

Dear Mom and Dad,

My last letter before vacation! When I'm not cramming for finals, I'm rehearsing for the show. I haven't turned into a superprep (yet), but at this rate, who knows? I'm not absolutely sure I'll make dean's list again, but you might put some champagne in the fridge!

Love,
Cary

It was the last class of the semester. I was sitting at the back of the classroom, paying more attention to the backs of the necks in front of me than to what Mr. Grady was saying. For some reason I was thinking about Madison. Two days before, he had left Winslow for good. I'd seen him in the parking lot, getting into his father's car. I hadn't liked him, but I felt sorry for him.

The bell rang, and Grady closed his book. "Best of luck on the finals," he said. "But no matter how poorly you boys do on the final exam, I won't be grading on a curve."

It was Grady's brand of humor, and everyone in the class groaned good-naturedly, as he expected us to. We slapped our books shut and began to make our way to the door for the last time that term.

"Billings, will you stay on a bit?" Grady asked almost as an afterthought. "You, too, Carmichael."

I didn't panic. I didn't have even the slightest trepidation. With Billings there nothing awful could happen.

The other boys filed out of the classroom. Billings and I stood in front of Grady's desk. From his briefcase Grady pulled out three photocopies and laid them in front of us.

"Take a look, gentlemen," he said. I looked forward. The one on the left was a copy of the homework I had turned in the beginning of the week. Next to it was a copy of Billings's homework. The third was a copy of the homework that I had prepared for Billings to copy from. Billings and I looked closer at the three sheets than was necessary for each of us to know what was lying in front of us.

"The third copy is the gift of an anonymous donor," Grady said as he pointed to the copy I had made for Billings. "It was left in my cubbyhole in the faculty lounge the other day. The others I made myself."

Billings and I nodded uncertainly.

"There's no point denying that sheet is in your handwriting, Carmichael," Mr. Grady said. "After thirty years of reading schoolboys' papers, I'm a pretty fair judge of handwriting. It's yours. You know it. I know it. Don't make matters worse by denying it."

"I don't deny it, sir," I said.

"I suppose you could tell me this is just a draft for what you did turn in," he said.

I said nothing. I knew a trick question when I heard one.

"It's curious, I admit," Mr. Grady continued. "Why, after all, would one's first draft have fewer mistakes than one's second?"

I folded my hands behind my back. My hands were sweaty.

Mr. Grady gazed at me, a half smile on his face. I unclasped my hands and let them hang down beside me. Mr. Grady turned to Billings. "Anything to say?" he asked.

Billings shifted from one foot to the other.

"Well, there's something to be said for being a fine copyist, I suppose," Mr. Grady said. "But I'm afraid you've proved yourself too adept at your task, Billings. You've ended up hanging yourself. There's not a comma that doesn't duplicate what Carmichael wrote out. I've checked and I've double-checked. I've hoped it wasn't so."

"I was very concerned about Madison," Billings said. "Carmichael was too. I had to spend the evening with Madison, talking to him about the joint he'd lighted up. There wasn't time for me to do my homework on my own. What happened was all my responsibility. I talked Carmichael into it. He just went along."

"Carmichael's old enough to know better," Mr. Grady said. "But it's generous of you to take the responsibility, even though I can't let you take it all."

"I volunteered," I said. "Billings didn't twist my arm or anything."

"I'm sure," Mr. Grady said. "But that's hardly the point. What are we supposed to do about this?"

"It's a first infraction, sir," Billings said. He was smiling now, trying to make as little of it as possible. Mr. Grady ignored him.

"I rather doubt that," Mr. Grady said. "I suspect it's been going on most of the term. Ever since your French grades took a sudden turn for the better. I've no proof, but I dare either of you to deny it."

Neither of us spoke.

"And since I've no proof," Mr. Grady continued, "I doubt either of you will risk expulsion from the school. We're stiff about honor here, but we're not inhuman, you'll find."

"Thank you, sir," Billings said. I heard the relief in his voice. It calmed me.

"Don't thank me just yet," he said. "You boys will have to be disciplined. But that's for the Head to decide."

"Yes, sir," Billings said.

"Yes, sir," I echoed.

"You needn't bother to take the final exam. You've flunked the term. Both of you."

"But Carmichael has done his work," Billings said. "He's earned his grades. There's no reason to flunk him."

"No student who has admitted to cheating can pass a course. And you've both admitted it, haven't you?"

"Mr. Grady," Billings said, "it isn't fair."

"I know it hardly makes sense to you, Carmichael, having to take the term over again. Especially since you have a decided knack for the subject and your grades have been outstanding. But the school has no other way of impressing on its students the seriousness of this sort of crime. Perhaps if other schools were as rigorous, the world wouldn't be in the sorry shape it is now. I know you're in no mood to thank me. But when you're older, you may. Other boys in your position have."

I knew that I would never thank him.

"There's one other thing, Billings," Mr. Grady said.

"It's Peabody, isn't it?"

"I'm afraid so."

"You're going to tell them to withdraw my acceptance, aren't you?"

"Not quite," Grady said. "In cases such as yours we tell them only that you have flunked a course. Naturally we also tell them why. The admissions committee will make its own decision. We have no choice. Peabody would find out one way or another. If we didn't let them know first, it would damage the school's reputation."

"They'll reject me automatically," Billings said.

"I believe they review each case on its own merits," Mr. Grady said.

Billings stepped back. "Is that it, sir?"

"That's it," Grady said. "I expect you'll be hearing from your advisers this evening. I'm meeting with the Head in an hour. He'll decide exactly how you'll be disciplined."

Grady picked up the photocopies and put them back in his briefcase. He snapped the case shut and looked up at us. "You're free to go now."

I waited for Billings to move first. He didn't. He stood there staring at Mr. Grady.

"Leave us alone, Cary," he said. "There's still some unfinished business that Mr. Grady and I have to take care of."

"I want to say something too," I said.

"Later, Cary," Billings said. "It's between him and me now. I don't want you to stick around."

"You both had better go," Mr. Grady said, "before

either one of you says something that will make matters even worse."

There was nothing left for me to do but leave. Without looking back, I stepped into the hall, leaving them alone. I waited for a moment, hoping that Billings would follow. I heard his voice rising. He was pleading. I was too embarrassed for him to listen.

I walked down the hall, listening to the sound of my footsteps on the hard linoleum.

The quadrangle was empty. All the boys, except Billings and me, were at sports. This afternoon the Winslow Blue intermediate basketball team would do without me.

As soon as I got back to McKinley, I knew I would spend the rest of the afternoon waiting for Joe.

Chapter 18

There will be a final dress rehearsal for the show on Wednesday afternoon, 4:00 sharp. It is imperative that all cast members and understudies be there. No excuses! Miss Ferguson and I think you've got a hit on your hands. Break a leg!

—Allan Martin

I sat at my desk staring out the window. The rain was turning into snow, and the snow was dissolving as it hit the windowsill. By four o'clock it was dark enough to turn on a light, but at five, when the other boys were returning from their sports, I was still there, sitting in the darkness.

Joe came in. I didn't turn around to look at him, but I knew he was there. He turned on his desk lamp.

"What are you doing in the dark?" he asked. "Are you sick or anything?"

"I'm fine, thanks," I said.

"I hope the light doesn't bother you," he said. "I've got some studying to catch up on before supper."

"No photocopying?"

Joe pulled the chair out from his desk and sat down. He opened a book: a textbook, not one of his paperbacks.

"I asked if you had finished with your work in the faculty Xerox room for the term," I said. "Or are you just finished for the day?"

"They don't make us do the bursary jobs durin[g] exams," he said almost under his breath.

"That's very considerate of them, don't yo[u] think?" I asked. "In your case, though, I suppos[e] you'll miss it."

"Can it, Carmichael."

"At least, they don't make you work at night," [I] said. "You copy at night only when you feel like it."

Joe turned in his chair.

"You must be feeling very proud of yourself to[-]day," I said.

"Why do you say that?"

"Come on, Joe. You're not going to pretend yo[u] don't know what I'm talking about."

"You've lost me," he said.

"I'm talking about some French homework you of[-]fered to deliver to Billings," I said. "I'm also talkin[g] about the only boy in the school who has a key to th[e] Xerox room in the faculty lounge. And I'm talkin[g] about how a copy of that homework found its way t[o] Mr. Grady's cubbyhole."

"I've done nothing to be ashamed of," Joe said. "It['s] more than you can say for yourself."

I wanted to slug him the way he had slugge[d] Bobby. Only harder, much harder. Joe was standin[g] now, and I knew I didn't have a chance against h[is] height or weight.

"No matter which way you look at it," Joe sai[d] "doing someone else's homework is cheating. Eve[n] when it's part of the old Carmichael like-me-and-I'[ll] do-anything-for-you syndrome."

"And I suppose you have nothing to be ashame[d] about being the self-appointed moral conscience [of]

Winslow School. You don't feel bad about snitching on someone?"

"I'm not sorry I did it, Cary."

"I've flunked French," I told him. "I don't know what they're going to do to Billings, but they're going to tell Peabody. Proud of yourself?"

"I wasn't the one who cheated," he said, but he wasn't looking so sure of himself now. He was sweating a little. "I wasn't the one who lied, Cary. Why don't you blame Billings? He's the one who let you cheat for him. Or Bobby for setting it up in the first place? Blame Madison's father. If he'd got his kid into Peabody, Billings wouldn't have asked you to do the last assignment. While you're at it, Cary, why don't you blame yourself a little?"

"You lied to me, Joe," I said. "In case you don't remember, that's cheating too. You told me you would take the paper up to Billings. You didn't say anything about making a detour to the faculty Xerox room. You didn't mention that you were going to screw up a couple of lives on the way."

Joe wiped the sweat from his face. "I did go straight to Billings's room, Cary," he said. "When I got there, Madison was there, so I waited in the hall. He was going on about how his father was never going to give another cent to Peabody ever again and how he was thinking of suing the school. Billings kept sitting there, agreeing with every dumb thing Madison was saying."

"Billings was trying to cheer him up," I said. "It had nothing to do with you."

Joe kept on talking. He hadn't heard me at all. "Madison was saying how Billings had lucked out with you, Cary. Getting you to do his homework so that he could get a decent grade in French. And Billings was saying how sharp you are. He said you were the one who invented the name Hamburger Face for me. And Madison was saying no, it was Katzenbach. And Billings said no, it was Katzenbach quoting Carmichael. And they start laughing, and Madison was saying no matter how bad things got, at least he wasn't going to end up some Hamburger Face."

Joe stopped. He was as furious as I had been. He was also on the verge of tears.

"But I didn't call you that," I said. "It was Bobby."

"You let me think you had nothing to do with it, Cary," he said. "There I was feeling kind of sorry for you because you were some kind of patsy, and it turns out you set Bobby up. You set me up too."

"I never meant to set anyone up," I said.

"So I went to the Xerox room," Joe went on. "And I made the copy. And I left it in Grady's cubbyhole. And I'll be damned if I'm sorry."

"When word gets around campus, you will be."

"You mean old Hamburger Face isn't going to win Winslow's Mr. Popular Award this year?" Joe asked. "Gee, and I thought I had it in the bag."

"It really doesn't mean anything to you that no one around here will be able to stand your guts?" I asked.

"I didn't come to this place to be popular," Joe said. "That's something no one understands. I came here for an education. I came here so I could get on that ladder and start climbing up it to all the things that people like you take for granted. Coming to a place like this isn't your basic human right, Cary. It's a privilege. I hated Katzenbach from day one because he abused that privilege. Maybe it was because you

father's a college professor, I thought you wouldn't.
But you did. So it's more than being called a name.
You got that?"

"I got it, Joe," I said. "I got it."

So finally I did find out what Joe was about.

And I'd done it the hard way.

Chapter 19

I'll be stopping by your room
this evening. Be there.

—Allan Martin

Before dinner, word had spread throughout the
school that an emergency faculty meeting had been
called to decide what to do about Billings and me. I
suppose I should have been flattered with all the
"tough lucks" and "no one would blame you if you
offed Ripley with your bare hands" that came at me
from the other boys. But I wasn't flattered. I knew I
wasn't the innocent victim.

There was complete silence at Mr. Grady's table. I
couldn't help noticing that the seats on either side of
Joe were not taken. One of the seats had been for
Madison; the other, for Billings, who didn't show. No
one asked if he was ill.

"Rotten break your getting caught," Bobby said.
After supper he had been waiting for me back at the
room. "What are you going to do about Ripley?"

"What am *I* going to do?" I asked. "What happened
to *we*, Bobby?"

"He didn't rat on me, Carmichael," Bobby said.

"What happened to the old team spirit?"

"You've got to fight your battles on your own," he
said. "It's not as though he turned me in, is it?"

"Forget it, Bobby," I said. "I'm not asking you to do anything at all."

"Aren't you going to do anything either?"

"There's not much anyone can do," I said.

"Ripley got you into this mess."

"He helped," I said. "He wasn't the only one."

"Well, I guess no one made you do the homework," he said.

"You're right," I said. "No one made me do it."

The seven-thirty bell rang. Joe came in and took his place on his bed. Bobby sat at his desk. I tried to write my parents about what was happening, but I couldn't begin to explain it. Not then.

Twenty minutes before evening study ended, Mr. Martin came in without knocking. He asked Joe and Bobby to take their books to the common room at the end of the hall and study there.

Mr. Martin sat at the foot of Joe's bed. He didn't take off his overcoat. I hoped it meant his visit would be short and sweet.

"Are you going to read me the riot act?" I asked.

"As a matter of fact, I'm not," he said. "I'm not even going to start. It's Mr. Grady's feeling that you're probably suffering enough."

"Mr. Grady said that?"

"Surprised?"

"Shouldn't I be?"

"Grady's in your corner, Cary," he said. "He thinks you're a fine student. He likes you. If he could, he'd like to let you off the hook. It's just that we don't have much choice in cases like yours."

"Grady says I flunked French."

"It turns out you haven't," Mr. Martin said. "You're getting an incomplete instead."

"It's not the same as flunking?"

"It's as though you didn't take the course in the first place," he said. "It won't hurt your average for the term, but you'll have to make up for the lost credit later on. Spring term maybe. Or summer school. If you can keep your nose out of trouble for a while, there won't be any record of this incident in your file."

"I have Mr. Grady to thank?"

"You're not the first boy who ever landed in this jam," he said. "But we're doing our best to see it doesn't happen again. You're on social pro from now until the end of the winter term, I'm afraid."

"What's that mean?"

"No weekend passes. No movies. No dances."

"What about the play?"

"Sorry, Cary. That's out."

"What'll you do?"

"The understudies will take over for you and Billings," he said.

"They won't be as good," I said. "They're not going to be able to rehearse during exams, are they?"

"They'll have to. Otherwise, no Christmas show."

"I've let everyone down, haven't I?"

"Yourself more than anyone else."

"What about Billings?" I asked. "And Peabody."

"The Head called the dean of admissions at Peabody this afternoon," Mr. Martin said. "Billings is out."

"Does he know?"

"The Head is talking to him now."

"And that's that?" I asked. "It's his whole life. Don't people understand?"

"I spoke about that in class. Remember? Where you

go to college isn't going to determine the rest of your life. I know the pressures you boys are under. I went here too. But you can't let that first-choice college thing get to you. It's not worth it. The pathetic part is, Billings would have got into Peabody even with a weak French grade. It was all terribly unnecessary. All of it, Cary."

Mr. Martin stood up. "One more thing. There's no one on the faculty who doesn't know how this thing came to light."

"You mean Ripley?"

"I'm not mentioning names," he said. "The faculty hopes you won't turn this into a vendetta."

"The faculty encourages rat-finking?"

"We can't penalize someone for it," he said. "Any attempt to get even with whoever gave the copy to Mr. Grady—"

"Joe Ripley by name."

"I said I'm not mentioning names. Any attempt to get even is going to cost you more than you're prepared to pay. Get the message?"

"I can't speak for Billings," I said.

"I wished you'd learned that earlier, Cary," Mr. Martin said.

"I'm learning it now," I said. "In English and in French."

Mr. Martin patted me on the shoulder and left. Ten minutes later, when the nine-twenty bell rang, I was still sitting on my bed staring into space. Bobby and Joe came back from the common room. They were on the verge of a fight which they had been saving for too long.

"Proud of yourself, Ripley?" Bobby asked.

"It doesn't have much to do with me really," Joe

said. "You're the one who got Carmichael involved in the scam in the first place."

"Stop kidding yourself," Bobby said. "You're the one who squealed. You're the one who's going to pay."

"Don't try anything, Katzenbach," Joe said. "I'm warning you."

"You're an asshole," Bobby said. "Even if you *are* the class brain."

"When it comes to being an asshole, you could give lessons," Joe said.

"One thing I don't get," Bobby said, "is how you're planning on living with yourself after you've turned someone in."

"You think rules are made to be broken, Katzenbach," Joe said. "You can make all the fun you want of people like me, but where I come from we stick by the rules. I'm going to play by the rules, and I'm going to win by them. And if it works out, I'm going to have the things you take for granted. The only difference is, I'll have earned them."

It went on like that for another half hour. I heard what they said, but I wasn't listening. The crazy part was they weren't paying attention to me either. There they were at each other's throat about who was more responsible for my downfall, and they were treating me like I was invisible.

Chapter 20

Ol' Man Trouble won't come 'round today
If you'll just Charleston your blues away!

—From *Riviera Rita*

The worst part was Andrea. I was thinking about her that night when I went to sleep. She was what I thought about when I woke up the next morning. On my way to breakfast I called her from the pay phone in Main.

"There's something I've got to talk to you about," I said.

"It's something about Alec Billings, isn't it?" she asked. "There's a rumor going around about him. That he's been canned."

"That's not it," I said. "But he's in trouble. Me too. Can you meet me on the path after lunch?"

"You want to come over here? It's warmer indoors."

"I'll explain when I see you," I said. "The path's okay?"

"Sure, Cary. I'll be there."

By the time we met she'd heard almost the whole story from the other girls at Bancroft.

"You're a jerk, Cary," she said. "You know that, don't you?"

"I'm sorry," I said.

"How could you let something like this happen,

you and Billings?" she asked. I had hoped she wouldn't be too upset. I wasn't prepared for her to be mad.

"I'm not going to be in the play," I said. "Did you hear that too?"

"Yes, I heard it," she said. "Deacon's taking over your part."

"I don't know what else to say except I'm sorry," I said.

"No one's going to die from it," she said, "but jeez, Cary, it was supposed to be terrific."

"Deacon's going to be okay," I said.

"Not what I meant," she said.

"He's a nice guy. He's not going to screw up."

"Okay. You're hurting, and I'm saying all the wrong things. How long are you grounded?"

"Winter term," I said. "I'll probably have to go to summer school to make up for the lost credit."

"You mad at them?"

"Myself mostly. I didn't feel I was doing anything wrong until I got caught," I said. "Dumb, huh?"

"I already told you you were a jerk," she said.

"You were right too."

"Like I said, no one's going to die," she said. "And tomorrow I'm going to start feeling sorry for you. And I'll start feeling sorry for not having been a better friend to you now."

"Anybody else would be as sore," I said.

"I'm not anyone else," she said. "I'm supposed to be your friend."

"You can have second thoughts."

"I'm entitled, I guess. But I'm not going to," she said. "Since you're grounded, maybe we can meet here next term. I'll bring you a cake with a file in it. The whole works, okay?"

I watched Andrea walk down the path and disappear at the curve. It was there I'd told Billings I'd tutor him. I turned and walked back to Winslow.

I took my exams that week and spent the morning of the French III test sulking in the library. I thought I'd talk to Billings once more at least, but I didn't. I saw him at meals, but otherwise, he was making himself scarce.

The last night of the term I was alone in my room in McKinley. From the window by my desk I saw only a few lights shining in the other houses. Almost everyone, Bobby and Joe included, had gone to Bancroft for the final performance of *Riviera Rita*. Afterward, the schools were having a joint Christmas party.

If the show was running on schedule, they would be getting to the end of the first act now, when Andrea and I were supposed to be doing the Charleston.

There was a knock on the door. It was Billings. We hadn't talked since the last French class of the term.

"I guess you and I are the only ones left," he said. He stepped into the room and sat down on the edge of Joe's bed.

"They should be doing the first-act finale now," I said. "I hear the understudies are good."

"That doesn't make my day, Cary," he said.

"I'm sorry," I said. "I'm sorry about everything that happened. I wanted to apologize. I didn't know where to begin."

"You don't need to," he said. "I'm the one who should do the apologizing."

"If I hadn't let Joe take the homework, none of this would have happened," I said.

"And it wouldn't have happened if I hadn't asked you for the homework in the first place. I've tried to figure it all out, but I wind up getting dizzy from all the if-this-hadn't-happened and if-that-hadn't-happened. I'm the one who could have stopped it once and for all, and I didn't."

"I still think you're one of the good guys," I said.

"The funny thing is, I think you're right, Cary," he said. "The trouble is, I'm no hero. Some people like to think I am. And honestly I like to let them think it. I didn't know it was hazardous to my health. And yours."

"I knew what I was doing," I said. "Don't blame yourself too much."

"I won't, thanks."

"Are you coming back after Christmas?" I asked. "Someone said you weren't."

"Yeah," he said. "I'll be here. I'm going to become a regular role model."

"To me?"

"To myself," he said. "If some of it rubs off, I won't mind, though. Someday you're going to find yourself a senior here. And some little freshman is going to think you're a big man on campus. You're not going to know what kind of responsibility you have. Don't let the kid down, okay?"

"I'll try not to," I said.

"Merry Christmas," he said.

"Bye, Billings."

The next day, after my father had picked me up in front of Main, I tried telling him about what had happened. About Billings and Madison and Bobby and Joe and me and what we had done. It took awhile before the pieces started to fit. After I had got home, I even made lists of the pieces and put them in the cabinet with all the other lists I'd made up since I was eight. It's not funny, like some of the other lists, and I know I'm not ever going to look at it and smile. Still and all, I know it's worth keeping.